Amish Quilt Shop

Son's Amish ,

Expectant Amish Widows Book 4

Samantha Price

Chapter 1

Be strong and of a good courage,
fear not, nor be afraid of them:
for the LORD thy God,
he it is that doth go with thee;
he will not fail thee, nor forsake thee.
Deuteronomy 31:6

With a thud Bree's suitcase landed at her feet. She looked up at the taxi driver, quite surprised by his sudden change of demeanor. Was it because she'd had barely enough money to pay her fare? She'd been completely honest with him about how much money she had, and he'd agreed to drive her to the address she'd passed him on the slip of paper. If he'd miscalculated the fare it wasn't her problem.

Without saying anything further, the driver got back into his taxi and sped back up the road. Bree hoped she'd get a better response from Simon's parents.

Shrugging off the strange behavior of the driver, she stared up at the pretty white Amish farmhouse, wondering what Simon's family would say when she told them why she was there. She'd seen them in the distance at Simon's funeral but hadn't introduced herself and now they'd have no idea who she was. But if Simon was being truthful, they were very nice people. Surely they wouldn't turn her away.

Picking up her suitcase, she was glad she'd only brought the essentials with her after her parents had kicked her out. In the case were a few changes of clothes, her cell phone, a few toiletries, and her makeup. After she took a deep breath to calm herself, she headed to the front door.

Before she knocked, she put the suitcase to one side of the door so they wouldn't see it immediately. She didn't want to do what she was about to do, but she'd thought things through and there was no other way.

After one more deep breath, Bree pushed her hair away from her face and knocked on the door.

A few moments later, a teenage girl opened the door. When she saw Bree, she raised her eyebrows and stared at her.

"Hello." Bree was completely thrown off her game; she'd rehearsed what she'd say over and over in her head, quite expecting that Simon's mother or father would answer the door. "Would your mother or father be home?"

"My mother is home."

"Could I speak with her?"

The girl nodded and left Bree at the door.

Simon's mother came to the door and stared at her, before she said, "Hello?"

Mrs. Stauffer was a small woman and her face was quite lined. Bree guessed she'd be somewhere in her forties, but somehow, she looked older. Possibly the stress of losing Simon had aged her considerably.

"Hello, Mrs. Stauffer. You don't know me, but I knew Simon."

At the mention of Simon, Mrs. Stauffer's fingertips flew to her mouth. "You were a friend of his?"

"A little more than a friend." Bree took a deep breath and glanced at Simon's sister standing behind her mother. Her well-rehearsed script wasn't for the ears of a teenage girl. "Could we talk privately?"

Mrs. Stauffer looked over her shoulder at her daughter before she stepped through the doorway onto the porch. She closed the door behind her. "We can sit out here."

Right at that moment, Bree wanted to run, but she knew she had no other option; she had to go through with it. She sat on a porch chair and when Mrs. Stauffer sat on one herself, she began what she had rehearsed, "Simon and I were very close. I don't know how to tell you this in any other way except right out. I'm having Simon's child."

Mrs. Stauffer looked horrified and gasped with both hands on her cheeks. She stared at her for a while before she said, "No! It can't be."

"It is. I'm more than four months along."

"He didn't tell me." Mrs. Stauffer started

howling, which brought her daughter running through the front doorway to her.

The daughter looked at Bree. "What's wrong with her? What did you say?"

Bree stood up and wondered if it would be easier if she walked away.

Mrs. Stauffer screamed at her daughter, "Go get your *vadder*. Tell him to come here right now; it's urgent."

The girl turned and ran into the fields. All Bree could see was the full skirts of a purple dress and the bottom of her boots as the girl ran. The pounding of feet as she ran in the dirt throbbed through Bree's head causing her to cringe. Putting her hand to her left temple to ease the throbbing, Bree turned away from the running girl and looked at Mrs. Stauffer. Mrs. Stauffer was eyeing Bree's suitcase.

"Please sit." When Bree sat back down, Mrs. Stauffer asked, "Where do you live?"

"My parents kicked me out of their home when they found out about the baby. I have nowhere to go."

"How did you know Simon?"

"I met Simon at a club. We became good friends."

Her face soured.

"We were going to marry," Bree added, knowing that, just like her parents, Simon's parents wouldn't be happy about the fact that the baby would've been born out of wedlock if they had chosen not to marry. Even though her parents weren't religious in any way, they were upset about Bree's pregnancy because they had wanted her to marry Ryan Lexington, the son of a wealthy couple they knew.

"It's too late to say you were going to marry. So Simon knew about the baby?"

"He did and he wanted to get married even more when he found out, but then things didn't turn out well. I want you to know that his intentions were good." Bree looked up to see Simon's father striding toward the house and her heart pumped hard against her chest.

Mrs. Stauffer stood up. "I'll tell him what you

told me. Then we must all talk."

"Yes, good," Bree said in the wind because Mrs. Stauffer was already hurrying to her husband. Staring at her hands in her lap, Bree sat on the porch not sure what to do. It suddenly occurred to her that they might not believe her. It had never occurred to her before now that they might question whether their late son was truly the father of her baby.

After Mrs. Stauffer stopped speaking to her husband, he turned around and said something to his daughter who had been walking up behind him. She immediately turned around and walked in the opposite direction, away from them. Then Mr. and Mrs. Stauffer made their way toward Bree.

Chapter 2

And now abideth faith, hope,
charity, these three;
but the greatest of these is charity.
1 Corinthians 13:13

Mr. Stauffer's gaze flickered over Bree and then fell to her suitcase. "Come inside. We can talk there," he said.

Mrs. Stauffer opened the door, walked inside, and then Bree followed. The house was dark after being in the bright sun. She followed Mrs. Stauffer into a living room, which was immediately to her left.

Mrs. Stauffer sat, and Bree seated herself on the couch.

When Mr. Stauffer was opposite her, he began by saying, "My wife tells me that you're expecting Simon's child?"

Bree nodded and remembered what she'd rehearsed. "I am. We were in love and had planned to marry." When they both stared at her in silence, she added, "I'm here for two reasons. The first one is because I have nowhere to go. The second one is that I need to give my baby up for adoption. I thought I should ask you first if you'd take the baby since you're the grandparents."

Mrs. Stauffer glanced at her husband.

"You don't want the child?" he asked.

"I can't possibly. My parents have thrown me away and I have nothing to live on, and no way to keep the baby. I spent all my money on the taxi to get here." The truth was she'd stolen the money from her mother's purse to get there. "You see, Simon spent many hours telling me about his wonderful childhood with all his Amish friends and I want the same for my baby, well, for his baby too." She sensed a more positive change in the atmosphere. "My baby is due in four months."

Mrs. Stauffer burst into tears and Mr. Stauffer patted his wife on her shoulder. "You can stay here until we sort things out," Mr. Stauffer said.

Bree heaved a sigh of relief, but was disturbed

because she clearly couldn't read these people. "I can? Thank you."

"What's your name?"

"I'm sorry, I should have said my name. I'm Bree Fortsworth."

"I'm Joel, and my wife is Marie. Marie, why don't you fix Bree something to eat?"

"Of course." Marie stood and hurried away to the kitchen as she sniffled.

"Is that your case outside?"

"Oh yes, my suitcase."

"I'll take it up to our spare room. We must talk more about this and see what our bishop has to say. I've got to get back to work; people are waiting for me."

Bree nodded and watched Mr. Stauffer as he opened the door to retrieve her suitcase. He walked up the stairs and Bree listened to his footsteps as he walked overhead. When he came downstairs, Bree heard him go into the kitchen.

She listened hard, hoping to hear what they would say.

Mrs. Stauffer said, "What will people say?"

"A child is a blessing from *Gott*. We lost Simon on *rumspringa* but *Gott* has brought us a blessing out of our mourning."

Bree had learned from Simon that when an Amish person dies on *rumspringa* they are considered unsaved. Simon had intended to return soon so he wouldn't be lost, but he died before he'd done so. Their many conversations had taught Bree many things about the Amish people and their way of life.

"You're right. This might be *Gott*'s way of answering our prayers; he's brought us another child. She says she doesn't want it."

Bree heard nothing else and a few moments later Mr. Stauffer came back into the living room. "I'll see you later tonight, Bree, and then we can talk some more." He gave a small smile and left the house.

Bree wandered into the kitchen. "Can I help you with anything, Mrs. Stauffer?"

She whipped her head around away from the

stove. "I'm sorry, I've been crying on and off since Simon died. I find it hard to stop when I start." She covered her mouth with her hand, swallowing hard.

Not knowing what to say, Bree just stood there in the kitchen.

Mrs. Stauffer said. "No, I don't need any help. Would you like something to eat? I've got a meat pie that we had for the midday meal. There's some left."

"I'm not hungry, thank you."

Marie looked her up and down. "When was the last time you ate?"

Bree shrugged her shoulders. "This morning I think. I've never been a big eater."

"How about I fix you just a small piece of pie?"

"Thank you. That sounds good."

"You can sit down at the table." Marie pointed to the table and Bree sat down.

"I'm sorry to just turn up like this, but I didn't know what else to do. I didn't know where to go or who to turn to. I think Simon would've wanted me

13

to come here."

Mrs. Stauffer didn't say anything. She busied herself getting the food. When she set the plate in front of Bree, she sat opposite.

"Was that Simon's sister I met at the front door earlier?"

"Yes, that's Cora. Simon's younger sister, and then Simon has an older brother, Andrew."

Bree nodded and picked up a fork. She noticed that she'd been given no knife so she put the fork into the pie and it sliced through fairly easily. When she loaded some pie onto the fork, she said, "I was at the funeral. I didn't come and say hello because I didn't think Simon would've told you about me."

She shook her head. "We hadn't seen him for a whole year before …"

"I would be grateful if I could stay here for a few days until I figure out what to do."

Mrs. Stauffer nodded. "Mr. Stauffer said you could stay."

"Thank you."

When they heard the front door open, Mrs.

Stauffer sprang to her feet, and rushed out of the room. Bree only heard muffled voices, but heard enough to know that it was Simon's sister who'd come back to the house. Her mother told her to go upstairs to her bedroom.

Bree ate quickly and was finished before Mrs. Stauffer came back into the kitchen.

"Do you want some more?" Mrs. Stauffer asked when she saw the empty plate.

"No thank you. Would it be all right if I go up and rest? I think Mr. Stauffer said he put my suitcase into a spare room."

"I'll show you where it is."

Bree followed Mrs. Stauffer up the stairs into the first room on the right.

"Here it is. We have a bathroom downstairs through the kitchen."

"Thank you."

When Mrs. Stauffer left, Bree shut the bedroom door. She looked around the sparsely furnished room and wondered whether she was doing the right thing. Simon had told her how he'd been raised with loving-kindness, so her child would certainly be better off raised with them rather than her parents. Not that her parents would ever raise another child. Bree's ultimate goal in coming to Simon's family was for them to agree to adopt the child she was carrying.

Bree opened her suitcase and switched on her cell phone, careful to turn the ring to silent since she knew the Amish didn't like such things in their homes. She stared at the phone once it was on and then checked her messages. There were no texts and there had been no voice messages left.

It was clear her parents didn't care about her at all. They'd always been too busy with their own careers anyway to care about her; she'd been told on many occasions that her arrival in this world had been a 'mistake.' Her parents weren't fit to be parents and Bree figured her baby deserved better. Bree looked out the bedroom window, thinking about taking a walk outside since she didn't want to be stuck indoors for the rest of the day – it was better than feeling uncomfortable around Mrs.

Stauffer.

Mr. and Mrs. Stauffer hadn't seemed friendly but they would've been shocked by her arrival and the news that their recently departed son was about to make them grandparents.

She closed her eyes and silently asked Simon if he was okay with what she was doing. It was hard to know. For so long she'd gone back and forth in her mind whether this was the right thing to do, until finally she knew she had to make up her mind one way or the other and just go with it. One thing she didn't want to do was cause the family more grief, but she knew from what Simon had said that they had longed for more children. Bree hoped that her child would soon be welcomed into their family.

The longest Bree could stay in the small bedroom was an hour; she couldn't take the confines of the four walls so she walked downstairs intending to find Marie and let her know she was going for a walk.

When she was at the foot of the stairs, she saw

Simon's sister sitting on the couch sewing. "Hello, I'm Bree."

The girl looked up. "Hello, I'm Cora."

Marie walked out of the kitchen. "We've told Cora that you'll be staying for a few days."

Bree smiled at Cora, and then looked at Marie. "I thought I might go for a walk, if that's all right?"

"You can walk on the road or in the fields, but don't go through the back fence with the barbed wire; the Patersons have a bull in that paddock."

"Okay, I'll be sure not to go there." Bree walked out the door happy to be in the fresh air away from the dark depressing house. The house Simon had described was different from the one she was experiencing.

"Don't go through the fence with the barbed wire," she said out loud as a reminder. Her parents had always accused her of being vague and forgetful and they were probably right. One of their nicknames for her was 'airy-fairy.' And if saying something out loud would save her coming face-to-face with a bull she was happy to do it.

The dress she was wearing was cumbersome and not nearly as practical as wearing her usual jeans or sweats. She'd only brought large dresses with her because she didn't want to be disrespectful to Simon's parents. He'd told her that the Amish see pants as men's clothes and their women don't wear them. Anyway, she'd now grown out of all her jeans thanks to her baby bump.

Chapter 3

But they that wait upon the LORD shall renew their
strength;
they shall mount up with wings as eagles;
they shall run, and not be weary;
and they shall walk, and not faint.
Isaiah 40:31

When she saw an inviting line of trees in the distance, she was more than certain that they lined a river or a stream. There was only one fence she had to climb through to reach it, and seeing it wasn't a barbed-wire fence she slipped through it.

As soon as she'd made it through she noticed a cow staring at her. Not being comfortable with cows she walked quickly. When she heard snorts she turned to see that the cow wasn't a cow at all, it looked very much like a bull. She glanced back at the fence she'd just come through to see how far it would be to run back. Should she walk or should she run? She figured that if she ran the bull might chase her, but if she slowly backed away toward the fence, he might leave her alone.

She heard a male voice yell, "Don't move! When he turns to me, run for the fence."

Bree looked over at the man who was now waving his arms at the bull and yelling. The distraction worked and the bull had turned to look at the man. Taking advantage of the bull turning the other way, she ran for the fence.

Just as she slipped through, the man yelled, "Are you okay?"

She looked down at her arm that had grazed against a piece of wire that had been sticking out of the fence post. "I'm okay, are you?"

"Stay there!" he ordered and proceeded to walk around the paddock, in the opposite direction from the trees, toward her.

It was Simon's brother Andrew; she recognized him from the funeral. She wondered if he'd heard the news that she was visiting.

He reached her at last. "What were you doing in with the bull?"

"I was just going for a walk. I was just at your

parents' house. I'm Bree, a friend of Simon's.

He smiled. "So you're Bree?"

She nodded. "He told you about me?"

"He mentioned you."

"I'm staying at your house for a while. I recognize you from the funeral." She looked down at her feet and back up into his face. "I might as well tell you because you'll find out sooner or later."

"What will I find out?"

"I'm having Simon's baby."

He frowned. "You are?"

She nodded.

"And you've told my parents?"

"Yes I have. They said I could stay for a while because I've got nowhere else to stay."

"You don't have any family?"

"My parents have disowned me. They told me to move out of their home as soon as I told them."

"Your parents weren't fond of Simon?"

She shrugged her shoulders. "They never met him. They wanted me to marry someone rich, well, his father is rich. When I'd ruined their plan they had no further use for me, and that's how it always is with them."

He scratched his neck.

"I've been a nuisance to them from the day I was born. No, probably before that." Bree looked over at the bull, wondering why she was telling this man her entire life story. The bull was staring at the both of them. "I hope I haven't upset the bull."

"He's pretty docile. I'd say you've just given him a bit of excitement."

"When I told your mother I was going for a walk she said not to go through the barbed wire fence and there's no barbed wire anywhere."

He looked down at the fence and touched the top wire. "This is barbed wire – see, these short pieces are wrapped around the main wire, and their sharp bare ends are called barbs."

Bree's mouth fell open. "Is it? I thought it was something entirely different."

Andrew threw his head back and laughed. "I can't imagine what you'd have thought it would be."

"I don't know. I just thought barbed wire was that crisscross wire."

"You might be talking about chicken wire."

"Just as well you were around to save me."

He shook his head. "You might have been all right if you walked slow and didn't look like a threat."

A giggle escaped Bree's lips. "I'll remember that for next time."

"I'm sorry to hear you got that reaction from your parents. It must be hard for you. Do you have any kind of plans?"

She remained quiet and looked at the bull, wondering how much to tell him.

"I'm sorry; I'm asking too many questions."

"The only plan I've come up with after weeks and weeks of thinking about it is to find good parents to raise my child. I just can't do it on my own. From what Simon told me about your parents, they'd be the perfect people to raise my baby. I only hope that they'll want to do it. Your father said they'd talk to me about it tonight."

"They've always wanted more than three children."

"That's what Simon told me.

Since he was an adult, Bree thought she should take advantage of the time alone with him and get him on board with her plans. "The main reason I'm here is I'm hoping your parents will adopt my baby."

"Why would they need to adopt the baby if the baby is their grandchild?"

Bree bit her lip. "I don't want to raise the baby. I mean, I can't. I've got no money, this wasn't planned, and for a host of other reasons. If they adopt the baby I can walk away with a clear conscience."

"You plan to leave the baby here and walk away?" He drew his eyebrows together.

"I suppose I'll have to. Simon told me how wonderful it was growing up in his house and I want our baby to have that same chance. I'd be a terrible parent, besides that, I'm far too young."

He took a sideways glance at her. "How old are

you?"

"I'm nineteen."

"That's old enough."

"I've not done anything. I haven't lived my life yet."

He chuckled. "What kind of things do you want to do with your life that you can't do when you've got a child?"

"I don't know, but I've got no father for the child and that means that everything will be up to me; it's too much responsibility."

"What did my parents say?"

"They didn't say 'yes' and they didn't say 'no.'"

He chuckled. "They're always hinting for me to get married and I know it's only so they can have grandchildren. When they get over their shock, they'll be happy – don't worry about that."

"That's what I'm hoping for."

"There's no doubt about it.

"Do you work on the farm here?"

He shook his head. "There is no longer much money in running a farm of our size. My father has been a builder for around twenty years now, and I work with him."

"Just like Simon."

"Yes that's right. We're not working today because we took the day off to repair some of our fences."

Bree nodded. "And what does your sister do?"

"Cora stays home with our mother and looks after the house."

He looked about him. "Where were you headed on your walk?"

"I saw those trees over there and then I thought there might be a stream behind them."

"There is." He smirked and touched the barbed wire. "You can figure that out and you didn't know this was barbed wire?"

"I guess that is kind of odd."

"Come on, I'll show you the creek."

"I'd like that."

Andrew was similar in looks to Simon with his height, dark hair, and brown eyes, although she was beginning to see that their personalities were dissimilar. Simon had always been joking around and he was loud, but Andrew seemed serious and a more mature version of his younger brother. Maybe Simon would've been just like Andrew in a few years time.

"Do you mind if I ask you a few questions about my brother?" He glanced over at her.

"I don't mind; what do you want to know?"

"Were you with him when he died?"

"I was supposed to be, but I didn't feel well that night so I stayed at home. I didn't like him racing cars, but I didn't feel I should tell him what to do."

"Surely you could've if you were in a relationship?" He shook his head. "Ignore what I just said. Did you live together?"

"No; I lived with my parents. Simon lived with his other friends."

"Yeah, I met his other friends, most of them anyway."

Figuring it would make Andrew feel better, she added, "He was going back to the community, you know. He told me he planned to."

29

"Were you coming back with him?"

"We never got to talk about that."

"He did know about the baby, didn't he?"

Bree nodded. "He did." Suddenly feeling very uneasy talking about Simon, she looked up at Andrew. "I better get back to the house."

He stopped still. "The creek's not far now."

"I'm suddenly feeling tired."

He turned around. "Another day, then."

She smiled. "Yes, another day." Bree considered she'd done the right thing by opening up to him a little. He seemed firmly on her side.

When they got back to the house, Andrew took Bree around to the back door that led into the kitchen. His mother and Cora were busy in the kitchen and they looked up when Andrew and Bree walked in.

"Where's your *vadder?*" Mrs. Stauffer asked Andrew.

"I don't know. I lost sight of him when I rescued Bree from the bull."

Mrs. Stauffer's jaw dropped open and Cora

stopped peeling the vegetables and stared at them. Marie looked at Bree. "I told you not to go into the paddock with the barbed wire."

"Turns out she thought barbed wire was chicken wire, *Mamm,*" Andrew said.

With her mouth open, Mrs. Stauffer stared at Andrew and then looked at Bree. "Did he charge at you?"

"I'd only just got into the paddock and Andrew distracted him so I could slip back through the fence."

"I'm sorry, Bree. I thought everyone knew what barbed wire was."

"She's a city girl, *Mamm,*" Andrew said.

"You could've been badly hurt," Mrs. Stauffer said.

"But I'm not. Just a little scratch that will be fine once I wash it." Bree gave a little giggle. "I'm fine. Do you need any help in here?"

"You could help Cora shell the peas."

While Andrew walked out of the kitchen, Bree went to the bathroom and washed her hands and the scrape on her arm. Then she sat down at the table with Cora. "I've never shelled peas before." She picked up a pod and examined it. "How do I do it?"

Cora giggled. "I'll show you." Cora demonstrated how to pop open a pea pod and use her thumb to strip the peas from the pod into a bowl, and then Cora popped one into her mouth. "They taste good even before they're cooked."

Bree placed one into her mouth and chewed on it as well. "Not too bad."

"You don't cook much, Bree?" Mrs. Stauffer asked.

"No. I don't cook, at all. I don't think I've ever cooked. I did help Mom once or twice at Christmas time with peeling vegetables, but mostly my parents get food delivered."

Mrs. Stauffer pulled a face. "Delivered? Do you call a restaurant and it's delivered to the door?"

"Yes."

"I'd like that," Cora said. "Does it taste as good?"

"Tastes better than it would if I cooked it," Bree

said, which caused Cora to laugh.

Mrs. Stauffer put her hand to her head. "I think you'll have to finish off the meal, Cora."

Cora bounded to her feet. "Do you have another headache?"

She nodded. "If you need anything, Bree, Cora can show you where it is." Mrs. Stauffer walked out of the room.

"She gets really bad headaches," Cora explained when she sat back down.

"I hope that's not because of me," Bree said.

"She gets them whenever she gets uptight about anything. Sometimes she's in bed for three days with them."

Bree kept shelling peas not knowing what to say; she knew that her coming there must have been a nasty shock for Mrs. Stauffer.

"My mother told me why you're here."

"I didn't know whether to say anything or not, but I'm glad she told you."

"I'm glad it's all happened."

"Thank you, Cora, but I'm sad it caused your

mother to get sick."

"Don't worry. It doesn't take much to give her a headache."

"Does she take anything for them? Are you allowed to take medicines?"

"We can. We do go to doctors. She's tried dozens of things but nothing seems to work for her except sleeping it off in a dark room. A cold wet washcloth on her forehead helps," Cora said. "I'll go take her one now."

"I think drinking a lot of water is supposed to help too."

Cora stood up. "I'll take her a pitcher of water as well."

When Cora walked out of the room, the back door opened and Mr. Stauffer walked through.

"Where is everyone?" he asked.

"Mrs. Stauffer has gone to bed with a headache and Cora is taking some things up to her. I'm sorry, I'm afraid I might have brought it on."

"You need not be sorry," he said, taking off his hat and hanging it on the clothes peg. Mr. Stauffer closed the door behind him and walked further into the kitchen. "I'll go and see how she is."

Bree wondered if she should leave, but the only thing that kept her bottom on the chair was that she had nowhere else to go. If she did, she might have gone. Cora and Andrew seemed nice and friendly, but Mr. and Mrs. Stauffer were standoffish and it made her feel uneasy. Things weren't off to a good start.

It wasn't long before Cora was back in the kitchen, having delivered the cold cloth and the pitcher of water.

"She'll feel better now that *Dat's* home."

"That's good."

"Do you mind if I ask you things about my brother?"

"You can ask me anything you like."

"Were you in love with Simon as soon as you saw him? Or did the love take a while to grow?"

After Bree gave a little laugh, she said, "I liked him as soon as I saw him and then when I got to know him we fell in love." Cora seemed so innocent and young. Bree hoped that Cora wouldn't make a mess of her life. If she stayed with her Amish community she was unlikely to get into trouble.

"So you liked the way he looked? Both my brothers are handsome; girls tell me that all the time, but now I've only got one brother. I keep forgetting. It feels strange. I had two older brothers and now I've only got one."

"Simon's left a void in the life of everyone who knew him."

"I just wished he could've been around for a few more years. And come back to the community before he left."

Bree nodded and hoped Cora wasn't going to cry. If Cora cried then she'd be unable to stop herself from crying also.

"I hadn't seen him in so long. Sometimes I find it hard to remember what he looked like," Cora said staring into the distance. After a while Cora looked over at Bree. "I shouldn't be talking like this. You of all people must miss him the most."

Bree smiled at her, grateful that Cora was being so kind.

Chapter 4

For we are saved by hope:
but hope that is seen is not hope:
for what a man seeth, why doth he yet hope for?
Romans 8:24

Marie had to get away from Bree; she was too much of a reminder of Simon. She was just the sort of girl she'd imagined Simon would marry – pretty and vibrant, and with her blond hair and blue eyes, she was the woman she saw married to her son.

Once Marie took her prayer *kapp* off, she slipped between the sheets, longing for her husband to come home. Trying not to cry was something she was well practiced at lately, but today being faced with Simon's girlfriend and his soon-to-be-born child was reason enough to cry.

Tears trickled down her cheeks even though she closed her eyes tightly to try to stop them from falling. How she longed to see Simon's face just one last time. It was too good to hope that what Bree said might be true, but she had no reason to doubt her words. She wondered what her husband really thought of what Bree had told them.

Cora tiptoed into the room and placed a pitcher of water on the nightstand beside her. "*Denke,* Cora."

"Close your eyes, *Mamm.* I've got a wet cloth."

Marie closed her eyes while her daughter placed the cool cloth over her eyes and forehead. "Do you want water now?"

"*Nee,* I've not long had some." After that, she heard Cora tiptoe out.

Marie's thoughts were drawn back to the visitor. The girl was pregnant and alone; Marie's heart went out to Bree. Having no other choice but to give up her baby was a dreadful position to be in. She couldn't imagine being in her place and having to make such a gut-wrenching choice.

Maybe God had designed everything to happen the way it was unfolding. Was God finally hearing her prayers of long ago, asking to have another child? A grandchild would be a gift from God even if she and Joel never raised the child themselves. They could help Bree in some way so she could raise her own child. She wondered whether Bree could really give up her baby after the birth; she couldn't imagine any mother having to make a cold calculating choice that the baby would be better off with someone else. The young woman was showing a great deal of strength and determination, and Marie admired her for being able to put her baby's needs above her own.

For the first time since Simon died, Marie felt close to him. Having Bree and her child around would be a little like having Simon back. Part of him would be living on. It was a disaster having him die senselessly in a car accident, but maybe God had plans for Simon's child and Simon's death might make some sense in time. That's the best thing Marie could hope for.

Marie sensed someone in the room again, so she moved the cloth and opened her eyes to see Joel. "You home already?" She pushed herself up slightly onto the pillows.

"Jah. I came home as soon as I could. I thought you might not be taking the news well."

"It gave me a headache, but more than anything else, I had to get away by myself."

"I understand." He sat on the bed by her side. "I think her coming here is a blessing. Whether she allows us to raise the baby or whether we have our *grosskin* in our lives, Simon's *boppli* is a gift."

Marie smiled. "I agree. Of course, it's true. He has blessed us with another child in our lives even though it didn't come the way we expected."

Joel chuckled, and whispered, *"Gott* rarely does things the way we expect them. His ways are higher than our ways." He lifted the cloth from her forehead, his fingertips brushing her skin. "You feel hot. I'll refresh this and bring it right back."

When he returned, she said, "I'm shocked by Bree coming here."

Joel placed the cloth on her forehead. "It's a shock to all of us. Lie back and rest."

She lowered herself further down on the bed.

"Well what do we do now?"

"We can only wait. Wait to see what happens and then hope that the Bishop says she can stay with us for a time. I don't see why he won't. Many people have visitors, and not all of them Amish."

"*Jah,* they do." Marie took a deep breath and stared into her husband's face. There was something on her mind and she had to say it. "I've had a thought; what if this baby is not Simon's?"

Joel shook his head. "If the girl says so, we must believe that it is. She'd have no reason to cook up a story. If she wasn't certain, she wouldn't come here and tell us that it was Simon's. She doesn't seem a cruel girl."

"That's true. I shouldn't have said anything."

He patted his wife on her hand.

"She does seem a very sweet girl. I can see why Simon liked her so much. Bree's just the kind of girl I would have imagined him with."

Joel nodded. "Don't upset yourself by worrying about things."

"Will you stay by me and have dinner up here?"

"If that's what you want. We'll let Bree settle in with Andrew and Cora since they're closer to her age."

"Jah. That sounds *gut."*

"Are you well enough to eat a little?"

"I think I am. I don't have a really bad headache I think it's more shock and surprise that's made me feel so poor. Joel, do you think this could be an answer to our prayers?"

"Gott does answer prayers even if He takes a long time.

Marie sighed. "This time it has been long. I was just so shocked to see her standing there almost as though I knew what she was going to say. Do you think that's odd?"

Joel shrugged. "It's not often we get a young *Englischer* knocking on our door." He leaned over, lifted the washcloth, and kissed Marie's forehead. "You stay here. I'll go and tell them I'm eating up here with you. Later tonight, I must go and talk to Bree, but I'll do that after the evening meal."

Chapter 5

Blessed is the man that trusteth in the LORD,
and whose hope the LORD is.
Jeremiah 17:7

Dinner that night didn't go any better. Mr. and
Mrs. Stauffer ate dinner in their bedroom,
and Bree had dinner in the kitchen with only Cora
and Andrew. No one mentioned the reason she was
there and dinner was mostly eaten in silence.

When they'd only just finished dinner, they
heard scratching sounds at the back door.

"That'll be Dusty," Andrew said, jumping up
from the table. As soon as he opened the door, a
golden retriever rushed in. Andrew caught up with
him before he bounded on Bree. "Settle down,
Dusty; mind your manners."

"He's lovely," Bree said.

"That's because you haven't gotten to know him
yet," Cora said.

Andrew knelt beside him. "He's a bundle of

energy and he's got a mind of his own. I've barely been able to train him."

"That's because he's not a smart dog," Cora added.

Bree looked at the dog who was enjoying Andrew giving him a neck rub. "Maybe he's extra smart; too smart for tricks."

"I'm not trying to teach him any tricks. We're struggling with sit, stand, and especially stay. He just doesn't listen." He looked down at Dusty. "Where have you been anyway?" He looked up at Bree. "He was with me and *Dat* in the fields and then he took off and wouldn't come back."

"He could've seen a rabbit or something," Cora said.

"Maybe." He said to Bree, "He's only three, but he still thinks he's a pup. Still acts like one."

"Everyone ready for dessert?" Cora asked as she rose from the table.

"Yes please," Bree had never been one to turn down sweets of any kind.

"I know you won't say no, Andrew. I'll go up

and get *Mamm* and *Dat's* plates and see if they want dessert."

Bree watched Cora walk out of the kitchen and wondered if Mrs. Stauffer could be that ill if she was still able to eat. Whenever Bree had a migraine she hadn't been able to eat anything at all.

Andrew left Dusty and sat back down at the table. "My father said he'd come down and talk to you after dinner."

"That's good; that'll make me feel a little better."

"They're glad you've come, so you don't need to be worried about that."

"I'm not worried." Bree did her best to smile.

He chuckled. "Well, you do look a little worried, unless you go around with a permanent frown on your face."

"I've been very stressed these past few weeks with wondering what to do with the baby."

"It can't be easy I'd imagine."

"What can't?"

"To be in your situation."

"It's not easy at all. I never thought this would

happen to me. It was always something that only happens to other people."

"It was a shock to us all when Simon left us. It's been especially difficult for my parents because he died on his *rumspringa* which was probably their worst fear with him being away."

Bree knew their beliefs so she nodded sympathetically. "Your parents believe he won't enter God's kingdom."

"That's right. If he'd come home and been baptized into our faith, that would've been an entirely different thing and my parents wouldn't be grieving so hard."

"Maybe I shouldn't have come."

"You've done right to come here. This will bring my parents happiness. They're just getting used to the idea. Trust me," he said.

Cora came back into the room with two empty plates. "They don't want dessert so it's just us."

Cora dished out apple pie and cream and then sat at the table with them while Dusty sat down looking at everyone eating.

"This is the best apple pie I've ever had in my life," Bree said to Cora.

Cora giggled. "I'll show you how to make it if you want."

"I doubt mine will taste like this even if you show me how to do it." Bree had never been interested in cooking, but what else was she going to do while she was here? There was no electricity, no Internet, and no television. "I'd like you to teach me. I can always give it a go."

Cora smiled at her.

When they finished dessert Cora refused to let Bree help with the washing up. Instead, she insisted Bree go into the living room and said her father was coming down to talk to her soon. Bree sat in the living room with Simon's brother, hoping what Mr. Stauffer was coming down to say would be something positive. She didn't think they would turn her out on the street with nowhere to go and besides, they had said that she could stay there for a few nights.

More than anything Bree hoped they'd agree to

adopt the baby. It just wasn't enough for them to be the grandparents because then she would feel a sense of responsibility and she wanted to walk away free and clear.

She looked over at Andrew who looked just as uncomfortable as she felt. He smiled at her and she smiled back. To make conversation, she asked, "Did you ever go on a *rumspringa?*"

"No, I never did. Cora wanted to go until Simon had the accident."

"Best she doesn't go."

"That's exactly what I told her."

When Mr. Stauffer came downstairs, he sat on the couch opposite Bree. "Marie has one of her headaches so we might have to talk to you more about this tomorrow, Bree."

Bree nodded. "Thank you for allowing me to stay here."

"You are very welcome," he said. "We normally have a Bible reading after dinner. You're welcome to stay and listen."

"I'd like that." Bree figured she'd make an effort

to fit in if she wanted them to allow her to stay there until the birth.

Mr. Stauffer looked at Andrew. "Go and get your *schweschder.*" Andrew disappeared into the kitchen and came back with Cora. Once everyone was seated, Mr. Stauffer opened his Bible and proceeded to read. His words in the old English Bible language were hard to understand so Bree sat there and did her best to appear interested.

When Mr. Stauffer closed the Bible, Cora stood. "I'll finish cleaning the kitchen."

"I'll help you," Bree said rising to her feet.

Core turned around to face Bree. "There's no need. I'm nearly finished, I just have to put a few plates away, and that's all."

Feeling awkward now, Bree said good night to everybody and went upstairs hoping she wasn't being rude or going to bed too early. When she walked up to the bedroom, she closed the door behind her feeling bad about all the upheaval she'd caused them.

It hadn't been her intention to cause any of

Simon's family stress. He had said that they wanted another child, so surely any stress she created for them now would be made up for when the baby arrived. One thing she knew for certain was that her baby would be better off being raised by Simon's parents than raised by her.

Chapter 6

He that loveth not knoweth not God;
for God is love.
1 John 4:8

The next morning, Bree woke up and listened to see if she could hear any signs of anyone being awake. She switched on her cell phone and waited to get a signal. The phone beeped when it turned on, and she saw there were still no messages. The time on the screen was nine o'clock. After she turned it off, she pushed it to the bottom of her bag.

Bree changed into her dress and headed downstairs certain she'd see someone in the kitchen. Another thing Simon had told her about his family was that they were early risers. When she walked into an empty kitchen, she headed to the window and looked outside. Mrs. Stauffer and Cora were both outside digging about in their garden.

She walked outside to join them. "I hope you're

feeling better, Mrs. Stauffer."

Mrs. Stauffer looked up. "I am, thank you, a lot better. Come inside and I'll fix you some breakfast."

"We thought you'd never wake up," Cora blurted out.

"I'm sorry, I didn't realize it was so late."

Mrs. Stauffer was nearly inside, so Bree followed her.

When they were both in the kitchen, Mrs. Stauffer said, "Have a seat."

Bree sat down while Cora kept working outside. It was a perfect opportunity to talk to Mrs. Stauffer in private. "I didn't come here to cause you upset or concern. I can't keep my baby and from what Simon said about you and his life here, you'd be the perfect people to raise my baby." She didn't want to offend Marie by talking about abortion, but Bree had considered it, and then dismissed it. It was too late for that now anyway. "I can't keep my baby and I want to know that he or she will have a good life."

Mrs. Stauffer nodded. "If you truly can't keep

this baby that Simon and you made together we would be only too happy to raise the baby as our grandchild.

That was only half of what Bree wanted to hear; she'd still be morally and legally responsible for the child. A full adoption was what was best. "It makes me happy to hear that, but would you be the legal guardians and adopt the baby properly?"

"Is that really what you want?"

"Yes, I've thought the whole thing through and it's the best for the baby."

"Why don't you wait until after the baby is born and see how you feel?"

Bree shook her head. "I can't do that. I need to make a decision with my head and not my heart. And if I know now that you'll adopt the baby, I can switch my feelings off and the whole thing will be easier for me."

"We should all talk; you, me, and Mr. Stauffer when he gets home." She turned her back to Bree, leaned down and took a frying pan out of a cupboard. Once she turned back to Bree, she said,

"Now, we had pancakes for breakfast so would you like the same, with maple syrup?"

"Thank you, that would be lovely."

"And coffee?"

"I can't drink coffee anymore. It makes me feel a little sick in the tummy."

"Hot nettle tea?"

"That sounds like it would be good. Thank you."

As Mrs. Stauffer used a wooden spoon to mix the batter in a bowl, she muttered, "I don't know why Simon wouldn't have brought you around to meet us especially since he was coming back to the community."

Bree shrugged. "I really don't know. I think he might have been ashamed how it all happened."

After Mrs. Stauffer put the first pancake in the pan, she sat down with Bree. "Why didn't he marry you right away when you both found out?"

"My parents are strict. They wanted me to marry someone else and I never told them about the baby until just recently." She looked down at the table hoping she'd deflected the question. "And that's when they threw me out of the house."

At the sound of the pan sizzling, Mrs. Stauffer rose to her feet and then flipped the pancake over.

"It smells good," Bree said, suddenly hungry.

Mrs. Stauffer stood over the pan with the spatula up in the air. "And when is the baby due?"

"Around four months time."

"You don't look that far along."

"I know, but I am."

Mrs. Stauffer poured the tea and placed a cup in front of her.

"I'm wondering if I might be able to stay here until the baby is born? I only ask because I've got nowhere else to go. I'll help out with chores and things, and what I don't know how to do I'll learn."

"Mr. Stauffer is talking to our bishop about the situation today, so we'll see what he says when he gets home."

"Where do your husband and Andrew work? I know they're builders."

"My husband works in different places depending on where the work is. They're building a house now at the edge of town about twenty minutes away. Sometimes he works in his office in the barn, but that's only paperwork."

Bree nodded and remembered that Simon said that his family had a phone in the barn and not in their house. "Thank you," Bree said when she looked down and saw the tea in front of her. She took a sip to warm herself; it tasted like a weak herbal tea, which, of course, was what it was. "I've never had this before. It tastes good."

"Cora makes it out of wild nettles."

The thought of drinking hot liquid strained through weeds made the drink unappetizing.

"Are you very hungry?"

"I am now, it smells so good."

Before long, Bree was eating her way through the stack of pancakes in front of her. "These are totally delicious," she said to Mrs. Stauffer, who was sitting at the same table.

"You've already eaten I guess?" Bree asked, more for conversation than anything else.

"Yes, Cora and I get up early and make breakfast

to send Mr. Stauffer and Andrew off with a good meal."

Bree nodded and hoped her child would be a boy. The Amish had very defined roles, and even though there were many good things about their lifestyle, Bree wondered if the men didn't have it slightly better.

"Shall I help you with something today?" Bree wasn't normally a helpful girl but there was nothing else to do around the place; she couldn't just sit around and do nothing.

"Cora and I are doing the garden. We're weeding; you can come out and talk to us if you'd like."

"I don't mind helping."

"No. You don't have to."

"I'd like to, but you'd have to tell me which ones are the weeds."

Mrs. Stauffer laughed. "You don't know about fences, shelling peas, or weeds. We might be able to teach you a few things if you stay long enough."

Bree laughed and then took another mouthful of tea.

"Bree, there are some things I'd like to talk to you about." Mrs. Stauffer moved to sit closer to Bree.

"I'll tell you whatever you want to know."

"I didn't even see him for a whole year before he died and I just wonder what he was like in that year; he would've grown up considerably."

"How I knew him was as my best friend. We liked each other immediately. He was funny, lively, and kind." Bree giggled when his laughing face came into her mind. "He always made me laugh."

"He was always a joker. He loved to play pranks on people and always saw the funny side of things.

Bree nodded. "And he did like cars. I think that's the main reason he stayed away from the community. He and his group of friends all raced cars." Bree hoped she wasn't saying things that would make Mrs. Stauffer sadder than she already was. "I'm not sure what else to tell you; he was just Simon. Another thing I can tell you is he was always there for me, he always had my back."

Mrs. Stauffer tilted her head to the side. "What

does 'had your back' mean exactly?"

"He was always on my side with everything and would defend me if he had to."

Mrs. Stauffer nodded. "Sounds like he was the same boy that I knew."

"Yes, I don't think he would've changed from how you knew him; that's just how he was."

"Simon was always the noisy one of the family. He always entertained the others by making up things to do." Mrs. Stauffer stared down at the table and smiled. "He'd make up games for the others to play."

"Andrew and Cora?"

Mrs. Stauffer nodded. "Back when they were growing up we had no close neighbors. The three of them always used to play together."

"From what Simon told me he was close to you and your husband as well as Cora and Andrew."

Mrs. Stauffer looked across at Bree. "I hope it's not upsetting you, having me ask you questions about him?"

"No, not at all. I was worried that I was upsetting

you."

She shook her head. "I just like hearing about him because I didn't see him in that last year; he didn't come home. Now I wonder why he didn't want to see us."

"Would he have been welcome to visit on a *rumspringa?*"

She nodded. *"Jah.* That wasn't the reason."

"Perhaps he wasn't ready to come home and if he visited he might not have wanted to leave?"

"Could be."

"That must've been it because he talked about you guys all the time. He told me all about your family and what a good life he had growing up. That's why I wanted my baby, our baby, raised here with you."

"You must be certain this is what you want."

"I'm certain. What else do you want to know about Simon?"

"I miss him so much."

As Mrs. Stauffer's face contorted, trying to stop more tears from falling, Bree searched her mind for words of comfort. What could she say to this woman who was in so much pain?

"Perhaps when Simon's child is born, you'll feel better?"

Mrs. Stauffer blinked hard a couple of times then nodded. "Perhaps." Mrs. Stauffer smiled. "I'm glad you've come to us Bree. Simon would've wanted us to meet you."

Bree felt her whole body brighten up. Mrs. Stauffer seemed genuinely happy to have her there.

The rest of the day, Bree followed Cora and Mrs. Stauffer around helping wherever she could. Surely this would make Mrs. Stauffer see that she was a good person and that had to help in their decision whether to let her stay there or not.

By the time Andrew and Mr. Stauffer came home, Bree had worked herself up into a nervous state. Dinner was polite, with conversation about the gardening they'd done and what work Andrew and his father had done.

After dinner, Mr. Stauffer instructed Cora to stay in the kitchen while the rest of them moved into the living room. Bree sat on a chair and Andrew joined his parents on the couch. There was an awkward silence while Mr. and Mrs. Stauffer looked at each other.

"Marie tells me you'd like to stay here a while," Mr. Stauffer finally said.

Dusty walked over to her and nudged her hand. "I don't want to put you out, but I would be grateful if I could stay here." She patted Dusty.

"You can stay here for as long as you like. Stay here until you have your baby and you can see how we live. Then you can judge if that's how you'd like your baby raised."

Bree studied Mr. Stauffer's face, and then looked at Mrs. Stauffer. "So does that mean you agree that you will take the baby?"

Mrs. Stauffer said, "As long as that's what you decide to do after the baby is born. The baby will always be our grandchild, but if you don't want to raise your baby then we'll be happy to raise Simon's child."

Bree suddenly felt lightheaded and she sank

back into the chair. When she found her voice, she said, "Thank you, I'm so relieved." In Bree's mind, things couldn't have gone better; this was exactly what she wanted. She glanced over at Andrew trying to gauge what he thought of the whole thing. He seemed to be deep in thought because his eyes had glazed over and he was shifting around on the couch looking uncomfortable.

"*Gott* has blessed us with a grandchild," Mr. Stauffer said to Bree.

Bree nodded. "And is your bishop okay that I stay here?"

Andrew and Mrs. Stauffer looked at Mr. Stauffer, waiting for him to answer.

"He is. He knows the situation. And do your parents know your plans?"

"No. They don't care about my plans because they don't want anything more to do with me or my child."

Mrs. Stauffer said, "They might come around and see things differently over time."

A memory flashed through Bree's mind of the

last time her mother had screamed at her to get out. *You've always been a disappointment to us,* is what her mother hollered at her. *You could've had everything if you'd married Ryan. Why couldn't you have had his baby instead?* Her mother's last words to her were, *You've ruined everything! Get out! I never want to see your ugly face again!*

"No. They never will. I've ruined their plans to marry me off to a certain person, so that's that, as far as they're concerned."

"Starting in the morning, you'll live as we do. You'll be up early with Cora to help with the chores," Marie said.

"Okay," Bree agreed. "Will someone knock on my door? I don't know any other way to get up that early."

Marie smiled. "I'll have Cora wake you when she gets up".

"That would be good; thank you."

"How much did Simon tell you about us and our community?" Andrew asked.

"Quite a bit."

Andrew nodded. "Tomorrow you'll see what our meetings are like. We hold them every second Sunday.

"I'll look forward to it."

"It's an early start. We get there at seven in the morning."

"Get there at seven? What time do we have to wake?"

"Around six. We have all the meals for Sunday prepared ahead of time because we don't do any chores on Sunday. It's our day of rest."

"We only do the things that must be done." Marie looked at her husband, "Is that all we need to talk to Bree about for now?"

Her husband nodded.

"I've got some women's things to speak with her about so we'll go into the kitchen."

Once they were seated at the kitchen table, Mrs. Stauffer wasted no time in getting to the point. "Have you seen a midwife yet?"

"I've seen a doctor. I don't know much about midwives."

"Have you thought about the birth procedure?"

The birth was something that Bree didn't want to think too much about. "My doctor said I'm supposed to book into the hospital a few weeks before."

"You've arranged that, then?"

Bree nodded. "I mean, I will, when the time gets closer."

"We usually have our babies at home with a midwife," Cora butted in.

Mrs. Stauffer turned around and spoke to her daughter. "It has to be what Bree's happy with."

"The only thing is that I don't have money for the hospital, but I might be able to get some."

Mrs. Stauffer gave a nod. "Let us know how much it will be."

Bree looked up at the ceiling figuring she might be able to break into her parents' house and find some cash. After all, she was their daughter and they should be the ones paying for it not Simon's parents.

"Bree?" Mrs. Stauffer jolted her out of her

daydreams.

"I'm sorry; what?"

"Let us know how much it will be. Mr. Stauffer and I will pay the doctor's, or the hospital bill."

"Oh no, I couldn't let you do that. I've got money at home; I'm just figuring out how to get it since my parents have most likely changed the locks, knowing them."

Cora pulled out a chair and sat next to Bree. "I could take you there as long as it's not too far away for the horse."

"Thanks, Cora, but it's too far for a buggy."

"Now don't you worry about anything; it's not good for the baby." When Mrs. Stauffer patted Bree's hand, it came as the first sign of warmth she'd seen from either of Simon's parents.

Bree immediately relaxed knowing that what Simon had told her about his parents was true and she was doing the right thing for her baby. "What should I wear tomorrow? I have another dress and it's fairly plain. Would that do?"

Mrs. Stauffer's eyes flickered over what Bree

was wearing. "Do you sew?"

"I learned at school, but I haven't sewn by myself."

"Cora and I will show you how to sew and we can sew you some dresses. You'll need some new clothes for when you get bigger."

Bree forced a polite smile. "Thank you." All her life she'd tried her best to stay slim so getting bigger wasn't something she was looking forward to.

Later that night, Bree lay in bed wondering what to do. She didn't feel right taking money from Simon's parents. It was bad enough that she was staying with them until the birth. The only thing for it was that she'd have to sneak back to her parents' house and get money. If there was no money to be found she'd have to take something of value so she could sell it. They owed her that much.

Chapter 7

Greater love hath no man than this,
that a man lay down his life for his friends.
John 15:3

Bree was jolted from a deep sleep when she heard a loud knock on her door. When she opened her eyes, she didn't know where she was for a moment. She sat upright in bed and Cora stuck her head through the doorway.

"Time to wake up."

Bree's natural instinct was to throw something at the person who'd woken her from a deep sleep, but she'd asked for someone to wake her. The best she could do in her groggy state was mutter a polite word of thanks to Cora. When the door was closed, she stretched her arms over her head and looked out the window. It was barely light and the treetops were swaying; it looked cold out there.

Not wanting to make the family late, she got out of bed and found her dress. Once she'd pulled it over her head, she grabbed her wooly pullover and slung it around her neck in case it was as cold outside as it looked. She rubbed her half-opened eyes.

"Now what?" Seeing her shoes near the door she slipped her feet into them, then drew a brush through her hair. There was no mirror to see what she looked like. All she could do to look her best was to brush her hair. Even though she'd brought makeup with her, she wanted to look as plain as possible so she'd fit in. After she figured she looked as good as she could under the circumstances, she headed downstairs and joined the family in the kitchen.

They fell quiet when she entered the room and Marie stood up from the table. "Bree, have a seat. We've got scrapple for breakfast."

"I'm not sure what that is, but it smells nice."

She looked at Andrew and when he forced a smile, Bree sensed tension and knew that he was not totally happy with her being there. After she took a seat at the table, Mrs. Stauffer placed a plate in front of her.

"Scrapple is made from meat and cornmeal," Cora told her.

Not only was there scrapple, there were also eggs and potatoes on her plate. "It looks like a fine feast. I didn't expect this, I thought there might have been a cold breakfast this morning."

"There's not much to it," Mrs. Stauffer said with a warm smile.

Bree smiled back at her and picked up her knife and fork, glad that Mrs. Stauffer was not as stressed as when she'd arrived. Seeing everyone had nearly empty plates in front of them she ate quickly so she wouldn't make them late.

"Andrew and I need to hitch the buggy," Mr. Stauffer said as soon as they'd eaten.

"We've got plenty of time, you don't need to eat so fast," Cora said to her.

Bree nodded, pleased that she'd be able to slow down and enjoy the food. She wondered what type of meat it was but wasn't sure she should ask. She wasn't certain if she'd finish it if she found she was eating rabbit or pork. At home, the only meat she ate was steak or chicken.

When Bree had finished everything on her plate, Cora took the plate from her and ran it under the tap in the kitchen sink.

"Okay, are you ready, Bree?" Cora asked.

Bree stood up. "Yes, I'm ready."

Bree walked out the front door behind Cora. She'd never been in a buggy before and wondered what it would be like. Cora sat in the middle of the backseat in between Andrew and Bree. Bree felt like a child in the backseat. She looked across Cora to Andrew. How did he feel about being well into his twenties and still living with his parents?

The buggy set off down the driveway. The air was fresh as it blew across Bree's face and the rhythmic beat of the horse's hooves soothed her nerves. They hadn't gone far up the road when they turned into another driveway.

"This is the Millers' house where the meeting is being held today," Cora explained.

Bree looked at the buggies lined up in a row

not far from the house. "How many people are coming?"

"We normally have around one hundred and fifty people," Andrew said.

The buggy traveled a little farther and pulled in-line at the end of the row of buggies. Simon had told her nothing of the Sunday meetings and Bree was intrigued to see what they were like.

When they got out of the buggy, Cora leaned in close. "You can stay by me."

"Thank you. I'm a little nervous. I've never been to a church except for weddings."

"There's nothing to be nervous about." Cora walked toward the house and Bree walked alongside.

Mrs. Stauffer caught up to them. "I'll take you to meet the bishop when the meeting's over, Bree."

"Yes. I'd like to meet him."

"Bree's going to sit with me, *Mamm.*"

Marie nodded.

"I always sit at the back row," Cora said to Bree.

"That sounds perfect to me." Bree looked at

the crowds of people heading into the house and considered they would have to sit fairly close together so they could all fit in.

Once they stepped inside, Bree kept her head down as she walked to the back of the room with Cora. They sat on a long wooden bench with no back. Bree had imagined she might be able to relax or doze off but how could she? She'd most likely topple off the bench if she did. Bree stifled a yawn; she wasn't used to waking up so early. If she were home, she wouldn't have gotten out of bed until twelve on a Sunday.

Once the place was filled to capacity, a man stood and led the congregation in a song in German. Even though she'd studied German at school, she could only pick up a few words here and there.

"That's the bishop," Cora whispered to Bree when a man with a long black beard stood at the front of the room.

After a prayer was said, the bishop began his sermon. He was a little hard to understand which caused Bree's mind to wander. Looking over the crowd of people, she wondered who these people were, and what their lives were like. It was impossible to see who was married and who wasn't, as none of the couples sat together. Women sat on one side and men on the other.

Simon had never mentioned how tedious and formal the Sunday meetings were. He'd obviously only told her about the good things the community offered. Taking another look at the men's side, Andrew caught her eye. Staring at his head, which was turned slightly to one side, she noticed his profile was exactly like Simon's. He had the same straight nose, which was neither too big nor too small, and the same strong jawline.

Then, Bree's eyes wandered to the other side at the younger women. She couldn't get a look at their faces, but from what she'd already noticed they were all plain-looking women. Plenty of people had told Bree that she was an attractive girl, so she knew that was true, but she wondered if she looked all right with no makeup and dressed in hideous clothes.

Lost in a world of jumbled thoughts, Bree jumped when Cora jabbed her arm. "Come on, we can go out now; it's over."

"Oh good," Bree said without thinking, which caused Cora to giggle.

"If we hurry, we can get out first before the old ladies come to talk with us. Follow me." Cora took the lead and Bree followed close behind until they were safely out of the house and away from the crowd.

"What's wrong with the old ladies?"

Cora giggled. "Nothing really, but they'll tell me how much I've grown, even though I'm sure I've stopped growing by now. They've said the same thing since I was five-years old."

"I guess everyone's wondering who I am."

"Yes they'll all want to know who you are. They won't ask you or anything. They'll just ask around until they find someone who knows. Let's go and get a drink."

Making sure not to let her new guide out of her sight, Bree stayed close. Cora poured Bree a drink, and then got one for herself.

Bree took a mouthful and then noticed Andrew talking to a small light-haired girl just outside the house. "Is that your brother's girlfriend?"

Cora giggled. "No! That's Cilla Jones. Her brother is a friend of his, and he's broken his leg. I'd say Andrew is only finding out how he is. Andrew doesn't have a girlfriend. He had one once."

Her interest was piqued. "What happened?" Bree took a sip of her soda, pleased to hear some gossip.

"He doesn't know that I knew about it, but he took Michelle Fuller home from a singing a few times, and then nothing."

"They mustn't have got along, then."

"*Mamm* thinks he's too fussy, that's what she said."

"I suppose when it's right, then you just know."

Cora smiled. "Like you and Simon?"

"Yes. Just like me and Simon."

As more people came out of the house, Cora took Bree over to one side of the yard. They stood looking at the crowd and then Cora suddenly waved to a girl around her age.

"Is that your friend?" Bree asked.

"That's Becky, she's my best friend."

"Why isn't she coming over?"

"She's shy. She's always been that way with people she doesn't know."

"You don't have to stay with me. Go and be with your friends."

"No! I can't leave you by yourself."

Bree laughed. "I'll be fine."

"I can't." Cora stared across at Becky who joined another group of girls.

It was obvious to Bree she wanted to join them. "Did someone tell you to stay with me?"

"Andrew said I should stay with you because you would feel strange not knowing anyone."

"That was thoughtful of him." She looked around for Andrew but now she couldn't see him anywhere. "I didn't think he liked me that much," she said more to herself than to Cora.

"He does. He likes everyone."

As Bree was looking for Andrew, she saw Mr. Stauffer walking toward them with the bishop. Nerves gnawed at her stomach. "I guess you can go be with your friends now because it looks like the bishop's coming to talk with me."

Cora took a step away. "You don't mind?"

"Of course not. Go be with your friends."

No sooner had Cora walked away than the two men were standing in front of Bree.

"This is our bishop, Bree. Bishop Michael."

"Hello, Bishop Michael." Bree put out her hand. "I'm Bree Fortsworth."

"I'm glad you could join us here today, Bree."

"Me too. I've never been to a meeting like this before."

"Joel tells me that you'll be staying with his family for a time?"

"I'm glad everyone's okay with me staying there." By the way the bishop's eyes kept flickering away from her, she was certain the bishop was a little unsure what to say to her which made her more nervous. Bree was pleased when Mrs.

Stauffer joined them.

The bishop said a few more words about Bree enjoying her stay with them before he and Mr. Stauffer walked away. Soon she was left with just Mrs. Stauffer.

"I understand Cora was told to stay with me, but I told her to go and be with her friends."

"Andrew was worried you might feel overwhelmed amongst all these strangers."

"I'm fine." It was just another thing she had to go through. A few more months with the Amish, and then her baby would be adopted by Simon's parents and she would be free. She wasn't certain what she would do after that, but one thing she did know was that she wasn't ready to look after a baby when she could barely look after herself. So far, her plan was right on track. In the next few weeks, she'd have to go home to find more money but she'd worry about that another day.

"I didn't realize so many people would be here today," Bree said.

"This is about the same amount of people we

usually have."

Bree thought back to Simon's funeral. There had been about three times more people at the funeral than at the Millers' house today. She was one of around ten *Englischers* who had attended his funeral.

Mrs. Stauffer turned to face her front on. "I know I didn't have a good reaction when you arrived. I want you to know that I'm glad you came to us. It can't be easy for you either. You must miss Simon terribly; just as much as we do."

Bree nodded. "I do; more than I can say. I really need him right now and he's not here." *Things would be different for me if Simon were still alive.*

Mrs. Stauffer turned back to face the crowd and was right by Bree's side again. "We have a meal now, and then the young people stay for a singing. Mr. Stauffer and I go home and then we go visiting. If you don't want to stay for the singing, you can come home with us."

"Is Cora staying?"

"Cora will stay on. Andrew will take us home

and come back later to collect Cora."

"I think I might go home, if that's all right. I don't know if I'm up for a lot of singing. I can't really understand the words anyway."

A woman approached them and Mrs. Stauffer introduced her to Bree as the bishop's wife. Bree was pleased to have a good welcome into the community even though they knew she was only a short-term visitor, staying until she had a baby that she would give up. She wondered if anything like that had ever happened before in the community.

Chapter 8

He delivereth me from mine enemies:
yea, thou liftest me up above those that rise up
against me:
thou hast delivered me from the violent man.
Psalm 18: 48

When Bree got home later that day, she walked up to her bedroom and turned on her phone. It beeped and she smiled, glad that she'd received a message, but when she looked at the screen she saw that it was only a warning-beep that the battery was running low.

Where could she recharge her phone? She heard the buggy leaving and knew Mr. and Mrs. Stauffer were heading off to visit people. Recalling what Simon had told her, she was certain that there was a good chance there might be electricity in the barn; after all, there was a phone in the barn, and she'd been told Mr. Stauffer had a small office there, too.

She opened the front door to see that Simon's

parents were nearly at the road, down at the end of their long driveway. There was no sign of Andrew anywhere, so it seemed she was by herself. When she stepped onto the porch, Dusty had been asleep, but he roused himself and wandered over to her slowly.

Bree laughed. "You look like me when I first wake up." She crouched down and patted him. "Do you want to come to the barn with me? Come on, then."

Hoping there wouldn't be any loose livestock in the barn, she pulled the door open a crack and peeped through. To the left were stacks of what she thought must be hay and to the other side were stalls. With Dusty by her side she walked further in. One stall had a horse in it and the stall next to it was empty. Once she walked past the stall where the horse was, she saw a small room.

"Ah, this must be the office." When she walked in further she saw Andrew and jumped. "Oh, you gave me a fright."

"Not half as much as you gave me."

"Did you hear me talking to myself?"

He laughed. "I did. I thought I was hearing things."

"I've got Dusty with me, so I was really talking to him," Bree said with a laugh.

"I'll believe you."

Dusty walked under the desk, slumped down, and closed his eyes.

"What are you doing in here? I thought you didn't work on Sundays."

"I was just straightening a few things out that I didn't have time for yesterday." He laughed again. "I should be the one asking you what you're doing in here."

Holding up her phone and charger, she said, "I just was looking for somewhere to charge this." He didn't seem as hostile as he had at breakfast. Maybe she'd read him wrong.

He raised his eyebrows and pointed to their phone. "You're welcome to use the phone anytime you like."

"I just need to charge it in case someone calls

me, or texts me."

Now Andrew didn't look happy. It was clear he was running through his mind who she'd want to be calling her.

She added, "I guess I'm hoping my parents might call me."

He stood up. "Whatever you do with the baby is your decision, but I just don't want to see my parents think they'll be able to raise Simon's baby and then have you change your mind, leave, and stay away from us. It would be dreadful if you kept the baby and then we never even see Simon's child." He grimaced. "Everyone will be happy if you keep the baby, if that's what you decide to do. I guess what I'm saying is that my mother gets very emotional about things." He waved a hand in the air. "Everything I'm saying is coming out wrong. I guess we'll just have to wait and see what you decide in the end."

"I've already made up my mind and I won't change it. Don't worry. So, do you have a power outlet in here?"

"No. We don't have electricity in here, just the phone."

She dropped the phone by her side and felt she was going to cry. Her phone was the only link to the outside world, and she'd been certain they would have at least one power outlet in the barn since they had a phone.

"I guess I could drive you someplace where you could charge it. The library's shut today, but I could take you to a coffee shop where you can recharge it."

She brightened up. "Would you?"

He nodded.

"Would we have to wait until your parents get back?"

"I've got my own horse and buggy."

"I'd love that so much. I'd be so grateful."

Andrew smiled. "I need to do a few things here, but I'll be ready to go in twenty minutes."

"I'll be waiting." Bree turned on her heel and walked out of the barn. She'd feel so much better when the phone was charged. If she only turned it on once or twice a day, like she had been doing, the charge should last for weeks.

She sat waiting for Andrew on the porch, wrapped in her pullover. The day had warmed up and the sun was warming her legs. Bree watched as Andrew led his tall bay horse out of the barn and proceeded to hitch the buggy. Dusty was now sitting outside the barn door watching Andrew's every move.

"Are you ready?" he called out as he got into the driver's seat.

She hurried over and climbed up beside him. "Thank you for doing this."

"Boris likes to go out every day; you're doing him a favor."

"Your horse is Boris?"

"No I call my buggy Boris." When she glanced at him he laughed. "Yes my horse is Boris."

She looked down at her hands in her lap. "I suppose it was a silly question."

"Perhaps I should give my buggy a name. I never thought of it before." He made a loud clicking sound with his mouth and the horse walked forward.

"Do you go into town very often?"

"Every other day. *Mamm* always seems to need something from town. *Dat* and I work all over the place so it's no trouble for us to stop in and get things. She usually needs some ingredient she's forgotten for the meals."

"I never grew up with home cooking. My mother never cooked."

He leaned back and looked at her. "Never?"

"My mother and father are lawyers. They've always been wrapped up in their careers. That's all that matters to them."

"What about their family?"

She shook her head. "I've never met anyone from their families, and I'm their only child. I think I remember my mother's brother, but then they had a fight with him too. They only get along with each other and they don't speak to any of their relatives any more. Now they've tossed me and my baby aside too."

"And now that Simon's gone, you have no one?"

"That's right. No one."

"No friends?"

"I wasn't raised with many people around and I guess that's why I don't have many friends."

"I can't work out why I never met you when I visited Simon."

"I don't know." Bree shrugged.

"He should've mentioned you as being more than just a friend."

"He would've in time."

"I guess."

"Where are we going?"

"I've been to a café that's just outside town on this side. I'm hoping they're open today. We can have something to eat or drink while we're waiting for your phone to charge."

"I have no money. I need to go back home and collect the rest of my money before too long. I can pay you back if you've got enough to pay today."

"I have enough; no need to pay me back. Is your home far from here?"

"Too far to go by buggy. I'll have to get a taxi

there one day."

"I would've driven you if it wasn't too far."

"Thank you, Andrew, that's nice of you to offer."

"It's just along here." Andrew said some minutes later, nodding his head toward a cream brick building with red awnings.

"Looks like it's open," Bree said when she saw people sitting at tables on the pavement outside. Suddenly Bree felt self-conscious being around non-Amish people while she was dressed so weirdly - with no makeup on and wearing a dress. She normally wore makeup all the time and, up until she'd gotten pregnant, had always worn jeans. It didn't matter around the Amish but she just hoped there would be no one there that she knew.

"Bree, before we go in I want to say something."

Bree's brows drew together and she held her breath in nervousness. "What is it?"

"Why not marry me?"

Chapter 9

O Lord, thou hast brought up my soul from the grave: thou hast kept me alive, that I should not go down to the pit.
Psalm 30:3

Her breath caught in her throat. This was the very last thing she'd expected him to say. When she saw he wasn't joking, she answered, "We barely know each other."

"I think you're a nice person and I should be married by now with my own family. Besides all that, it'll give your baby a proper start in life."

"Are you doing this for your brother?"

He inhaled sharply. "For his baby, for you, and for me."

She smiled. "I'm not Amish."

"You could join."

"I'm not certain that I even believe there is a God. I wouldn't feel right about being a member of something I didn't totally believe in." She looked into his handsome face and knew she might very well be able to fall in love with someone like him, but it wouldn't be fair to marry under such circumstances.

"Have a think about it?"

She gave a giggle and covered her mouth with her fingertips. "No one's ever asked me to marry him before."

He frowned. "Didn't you say Simon and you were to be married?"

"Oh, I mean, besides Simon."

Andrew stared at her, and Bree knew he had more questions. "We should go and get this phone charged."

After Andrew secured his horse, they walked into the coffee shop. He pointed her to a table against the wall, noticing that there was a power outlet underneath it.

When they sat down, Andrew took the charger from her, bent down and slotted the charger into the socket. Bree took the phone, inserted the cord, and set it at the side of the table.

"Thank you. It's getting harder for me to get up and down."

He smiled at her and was about to say something when the waiter brought them menus.

"Eat whatever you like," Andrew said to her.

Bree opened the menu. "I'm a little bit hungry. I didn't eat much today; I was too nervous."

"At the meeting?"

Bree nodded.

"There's nothing to be nervous about."

Nervousness was something that Bree couldn't just switch off. "I was nervous about the bishop speaking to me and what everyone thought about me. I know people can't be happy about Simon having a child without being married, and all that. I know they are upset enough that he died on his *rumspringa* doing illegal car racing."

"These are all things that can't be changed now."

"I know. I guess I just worry about what people think about me and Simon."

"Don't worry about what other people think. Do you think that you worrying about it will change what people are going to think?"

Bree laughed. "No. I suppose that's true."

He smiled kindly. "Then pay them no mind. People will think what they will and what does it matter? It's what you feel and think about yourself that you *can* change. You can never change another person."

Bree stared into his brown eyes and knew immediately he was a sincere and kind man. "Thank you. That's good advice. I'll remember that." Simon and his brother were opposites. Simon had been wild and crazy, whereas his older brother was wise and sensible. If Simon hadn't been so crazy he might not have gotten in his car drunk, and raced in that car race that night.

"What kind of things did you like to do with my brother? I suppose that's a personal question so don't answer if you don't want to tell me."

"No that's okay. We used to talk about a lot of things. He'd tell me about you, Cora, and your parents, and how he had so much fun growing up playing with the animals - the puppies and the baby chickens, all that kind of thing. Then we'd watch movies a lot, and just hang out."

Andrew nodded and looked down at his food. "Thanks for telling me. I often wonder what his last year was like. You probably know that I visited him three times, but it was only briefly. We just met up to have a talk for about an hour or so."

"I think with the car racing, he was getting everything out of his system before he went back home. He had a bit of a wild side."

"Did you like his wild side?"

Bree smiled and shook her head. "No. It was his kind heart and his goodness that I liked."

Andrew's lips stretched into a grin. He seemed to like her answer. "I remember he was always the one to make up the fun games when we were young. I guess he was the leader and Cora and I were the followers, which was strange since I was the oldest. I guess I'm a bit quieter and not as much fun as he was."

"Simon was quiet sometimes."

"How was he when he found out about the

baby?"

Bree sighed not wanting to bring back such memories.

"Again, sorry if I'm being too nosy," Andrew said.

"Not at all. I want to tell you as much as I can about your brother since we were so close in that last year."

"Did your parents meet my brother?"

"No they never did. They never wanted to meet anybody who had anything to do with me and I wasn't allowed to have friends to the house. They were just too busy with their careers and going to all their charity functions."

"That's very good of them. From what you said about them I didn't think that they'd be the kind of people to support charities."

Bree smiled and shook her head. "No. You don't understand. People like my mother and father only support a charity when it suits them. Charity events are social events and they like to be seen at them. They'll only donate money so they're seen to donate money. It's all about getting dressed up in expensive clothing and jewelry, so they can network."

"What do you mean by network?"

"Network is where they go somewhere so they can meet other people in the hope of meeting influential people who might be able to advance their careers; or meeting new clients, that kind of thing. They really don't care about the people the charity is going to benefit."

"Do you think they don't care at all?"

Bree smiled at Andrew's naivety. "They care nothing about the people the charity is helping. If they did, they wouldn't spend two thousand dollars on a new outfit to wear to the function – they'd donate that to the charity and wear something they already owned." She appreciated the fact that Andrew was trying to get to know more about her. "Anyway, I don't want to talk about them. I'd rather fill my mind with positive things." She noticed his well-muscled arms. "Have you been a builder for a long time?"

"Since I was about sixteen. I work with my father, so that kind of made it easy for me to break into it."

"Yes, I suppose it would've. I really hope I haven't upset your mother too much by coming here. She seems okay today, but it really worried me that I gave her a headache. I've had a few bad headaches in my time and I know how awful they can be."

"She doesn't take well to change."

"She's not the only one." The phone beeped and Bree reached over and grabbed it. "Oh, it's only telling me that it's now fully charged."

"That didn't take long," he said.

"I guess it doesn't take long, and the charge should last a fair while."

"I don't think my parents would like you having the phone in our house. I meant to tell you that earlier."

"I've been checking it in the house, but I've had it off mostly."

"I don't like to tell you what to do, Bree, but

modern things coming into the house …"

"Yes, I know, Simon told me about that. I won't turn it on in the house."

"Bree, I must be honest with you."

Bree put the phone back on the table and looked into his brown eyes. "What is it?"

"I'm really not buying this whole story you've concocted."

Chapter 10

I cried unto the Lord with my voice,
and he heard me out of his holy hill. Selah.
Psalm 3:4

Could he possibly mean he didn't believe that she was pregnant? "I'm not sure what you mean, Andrew. What story?"

"I've gone over and over this in my mind a thousand times. I'd say I knew my brother better than anybody in existence, and if he had a beautiful girlfriend, he would've told me. He did mention your name as the best friend he ever had, but he never mentioned you as a girlfriend."

She hadn't planned for this. Andrew could ruin everything. She opened her mouth to speak, but before she could, he put his hand up to stop her.

"Please don't tell me more lies. I just want to know the truth about my brother and why you're saying that this baby is his when you and I know it's not."

Bree gulped and then took a sip of her drink wondering what she should say and how she could possibly convince him that the baby was Simon's.

"What part of what I said don't you believe?" she asked him staring into his eyes.

"The only part I believe was probably the only part that was true; about your parents and your upbringing. I don't know who the father of your child is but I'm certain it's not my brother. What I don't know is why you're lying about this and causing my parents so much grief."

Her plan was unraveling in front of her. She picked up a paper napkin on the table and clutched it in her hand. "That's not what I meant to do. That's not what I meant to do at all. I was a good friend of Simon's and he told me what a good upbringing he had with your family. The whole thing sounded perfect and that's what I want for my baby. I wouldn't have thought of doing this if Simon hadn't told me that your parents had longed for more children."

"So you admit that Simon is not the father of

your baby?"

"Yes." She wiped a sole tear away before it trickled down her cheek. "I just thought it would be perfect and make your mother and father so happy if they could have another child to raise. The best thing I can do is give the baby to a good family, but I want to choose the family; I chose your family." Bree burst into tears and buried her face in the paper napkin.

"Don't cry. I won't necessarily tell my parents. Maybe this is a good thing for them. I guess if everyone thinks it's Simon's baby there's no reason for them to know otherwise."

She lowered the napkin. "Really? You won't tell them?"

He shook his head. "I had my suspicions from the start and I haven't told them yet. I could debate for days whether what I'm doing is morally right, but you're right about your baby having a good life. I can't think of better parents for your baby than mine. Would you keep your baby if you were able to?"

"No I can't. I just can't. Even thinking about it causes me to break out in hives."

"Who's the father?"

"He's the boy my parents want me to marry. His name is Ryan. I told them Simon was the father. Anyway, he's a lawyer too and the son of a very wealthy man. That's why they were trying to force me to marry him."

"Are you in love with him?"

"I thought I was until I found out I was just one of many women he's been dating. Now I want nothing more to do with him." She looked into Andrew's eyes. "Why did you ask me to marry you just now if you knew I was lying?"

"To see if I was right about you. I knew by your answer that Simon wasn't the father."

"I suppose you think I'm a terrible person."

He shook his head. "Just a person trying to do what she thinks is best."

"Simon and I were very good friends and I think he really wouldn't have minded about me telling lies if it was for the good of my baby. He was really my best friend, my best friend in the world. I miss him so much."

"He did tell me how close the two of you were."

"I'm just trying to right my mistakes, Andrew." As soon as Bree said the word 'mistake' she remembered that her parents had always described her as a mistake. She never would call her baby a mistake again; it was a horrible thing to say.

"Does this man know that you're expecting his baby?"

Bree shook her head. "No and he doesn't deserve to know. He's been lying to me from the beginning."

Andrew raised his eyebrows.

"I know. You're thinking I'm a liar too, but I'm not normally. Please believe me."

"I think the man deserves to know about the baby, before you give the baby up, if that's what you decide to do. Surely he deserves some say in what will happen to his child."

"I can't. If I tell him, he won't leave me alone; he's not a nice person and I'll have to deal with him for the rest of my life. My parents would be pleased if they knew it was Ryan's baby."

"You lied to your parents as well by telling them the baby was Simon's?"

"Yes. I've told you everything and I only lied out of desperation." Bree wiped her eyes hoping Andrew wouldn't think too badly of her. "I know this all looks like I'm a dreadful liar, but I just want to be free of people who don't have my best interests at heart."

"Surely your parents only want good things for you."

"No. They don't. They never meant to have a baby. I was a mistake and they let me know it all the time. They're both lawyers and they're always working. I think I told you that already, but their jobs are all they care about. They wanted me to marry Ryan so they can get in good with Ryan's father who's a multimillionaire."

"Even so, I'm sure they love you."

Bree shook her head. "Then why did they tell me to go when I told them I was having a baby?

Anyway, Simon told me that I shouldn't have anything more to do with him, the way he was treating me."

"Ryan?"

Bree nodded and then the tears started to fall again. "Now I don't know what to do. I've made such a mess of things."

Andrew reached out and patted her on the hand. "I'm sure things will work out."

"I don't see how they will. Everyone will know that I'm dishonest and I feel so ashamed of making so many mistakes with my life. I've lost my best friend in a car accident and he was the only person who understood me. He was like a brother and now I've lost him and I'm all alone with no one."

"I'll be there for you. I'll help you as much as I can."

She blotted her eyes dry with the paper napkin that was now quite soggy. "How would you help me? If I tell your parents the truth they'll hate me and never trust me. They think they're going to be grandparents and have another baby to raise, but they might not want to raise my baby if they find out the truth."

"Every baby is a precious gift from God."

"Well my parents never felt that way, and it certainly doesn't seem like I've been given a gift. It feels like I've been given a punishment. I want to do the right thing by my baby, but what is that—what is the right thing? Tell me, Andrew, what should I do?"

"I think you're right about one thing. It will upset my parents too much at this stage to tell them the truth. To find out now that they won't have Simon's baby around would be cruel, and would be like losing him all over again. You can't do that to them, not yet."

"Does that mean I should keep lying to them? Are you sure that would be the right thing to do?"

"I don't know. I think we've passed worrying about the right thing to do at this stage, don't you? I think it would be best if you keep playing along with what you've told them and see what develops over time."

"What do you mean by 'see what develops?' What could possibly develop?"

Andrew's shoulders slumped. "I'm not certain. All I know is that my parents will be too upset to find out now."

"Would it be better for them to find out now rather than be upset later?"

"Not if you continue in your plans for them to adopt the baby. I'm sure they would be happy about that."

Bree looked around the café and was glad that no one was looking at her crying. The place wasn't that busy. "Andrew, you've got to help me. What should I do?"

He rubbed his forehead and looked down at the table. "It's a tough one. Are you sure keeping your baby is not a choice you'd make?"

Chapter 11

*Let all those that seek thee rejoice and be glad in
thee:
let such as love thy salvation say continually,
The Lord be magnified.*
Psalm 40:16

"I keep telling you it's not, and besides that, I
can't. I really thought long and hard about
it. I had months to think it through, and this is the
decision I've made." *It's what's best for the baby;
I'm not being selfish. I think it would be selfish
of me to keep the baby when the baby can have a
better life somewhere else, with someone else.*

"I can't tell you what to do. I'll help you in
Simon's place if you want to go ahead with keeping
up the lies you've told my parents. I won't let
anyone know that I know anything different from
what you've told them."

"You'd really do that?"

"Yes, I would. I suppose no one will get hurt if

they never learn the truth. And if you were only going to put the baby up for adoption anyway, my parents would be the perfect choice."

Relief soared through Bree's body and she leaned back in the hard wooden chair. She had thought her plan was about to come crashing around about her, but now that Andrew knew, things might work out even better.

"Would you come to my house with me soon? I need to pick up some more money."

"Don't you keep your money in a bank?"

"Normally I do, but I left money in my room at home." Bree didn't like telling Andrew a lie now that he was helping her, but she knew he wouldn't go to the house with her if he knew she was going to have to steal money from her parents to support herself for the next few months. It was the only way she could get any money.

"Did you work?"

"I was between jobs and deciding what to do with my life. I don't think I'm the type to go to college and study. I have a problem with concentration."

"What did you do for work?"

Bree looked away, not happy about having to tell another lie. But how could she tell this hard-working Amish man that she'd never worked a day in her life and had been supported by the very people she'd been bitterly complaining about? "I'm sorry, Andrew, I just lied to you." She saw his eyebrows scrunch together and lines appear in his forehead.

"What did you lie about?" he asked.

"I've never worked. My parents gave me an allowance and it is true about me trying to figure out what to do with my life. All I know is that a baby can't be part of it. I just want to find something that I enjoy doing so I can feel fulfilled."

"What do you enjoy doing?"

"I don't know; it's hard to say. I guess I'll have to try a few things to figure that out. Do you like building?"

"Yes I do like building, but I'd still have to do it even if I didn't like it. You have to do something to bring the money in."

"I guess I'm just useless. That's what my parents say to me all the time."

He gave a little laugh. "Sounds like you're feeling sorry for yourself."

"I am totally sorry for myself. I'm in a bad situation, so I do feel sad for myself."

"Cheer up, you've got me to help you through. I'll be your friend and take Simon's place."

"You'll be my friend for real?"

"For real."

"That makes me feel so much better."

"When we go back to your house to get your money, will your parents be there?"

"I don't think so."

"You could try telling them the truth and see what happens. They could surprise you."

"They must never know."

He rubbed his forehead and shook his head. "I can't believe this is all happening. It seems we lived a quiet life until you showed up."

Her lips formed a pout. "Sorry! I feel bad about everything."

"There's no need to feel bad it's just that it's an unbelievable situation – this whole thing. I find it hard to learn that your parents don't care about you having a baby. I thought *Englishers* would be more accepting of things like that."

"My parents aren't like regular people."

"I haven't had much to do with *Englishers* but your parents do sound odd if what you've said is true."

"I'm not lying about them, Andrew."

"I don't think you were lying about them, at all."

"Oh." She looked down into her tea.

"Do you want me to get you more tea? That'll be cold by now."

"Do you have time?"

He nodded and stood up to order more hot drinks. She closed her eyes and for the first time since Simon's death, she felt a fleeting moment where she sensed peace. Andrew had said he'd keep her secret and be her friend. Maybe Simon was watching over her and had found her another friend. And if Andrew was willing to keep her secret, that's exactly what he was.

Andrew sat opposite her again and smiled at her. "Hello," he said with a big smile.

She smiled back at him.

"I can't imagine what you're going through right now. Going through all this on your own. Don't forget, though, you're not on your own now."

Bree smiled at him, glad he was doing his best to help her. It couldn't have been easy for him to make the choice to keep a secret from his parents. "That's how I feel; I'm not alone any longer and it's so good to finally share my secret with someone. I've been alone most of my life and Simon was the first person I felt I could truly be myself with."

"What was your friendship like with him?"

"It might have been an attraction of opposites. He was wild and crazy—the life of the party and I'm quieter. I met him at a club when he was there with his friends. Our eyes met and later we talked. It was like we'd known each other before; we talked until morning. I didn't even have anything in common with him, but it was so easy to talk with him. Nothing like that has ever happened to me before. I've never had an instant attraction to anybody. It wasn't like a boyfriend-girlfriend thing, it was like a brother-sister thing." She shook her head and looked at the table. "It's something I just can't even explain and it sounds weird to say it out loud. I suppose you think I'm doubly mad to be saying all these things."

"I don't think you're mad, crazy, or any of those other things. You shouldn't be so hard on yourself. If that's how you felt when you met my brother then that's how you felt. You don't have to apologize for it or explain it away. As long as it made sense to you and my brother, that's all that should matter."

She looked him in the eye and he made her see how apologetic she'd been for too long.

"Was my brother really that wild and crazy?"

"Yes, he was. He said he was getting everything out before he went back. His friends were a group of boys who liked to race cars.'"

"I know; I met some of them."

Bree nodded. "I was supposed to go that night

but I didn't feel well."

"It's a good thing you didn't go."

"I suppose it was. I just wonder if I should've told him not to race, but I didn't. There had been no accidents before." Bree stood up. "I think I need fresh air."

"Sure. We've been here long enough; let's go."

Once they climbed up into the buggy, Andrew turned it around and they headed back.

"My phone," Bree blurted out.

"Did you leave it?"

"Yes, I left it charging on the table. I switched it off when it beeped and left it there."

"Don't panic. We'll go back." They weren't that far from the café so he turned the buggy back around, and then stopped at the first place he could. It was not that far from the café. "You stay here, I'll go and get it."

"Okay," Bree answered, staring at the café. Considering the place hadn't been that crowded she hoped her phone wouldn't have got stolen in that short space of time.

Moments later, when she looked up she saw Andrew coming towards her and when he saw that she was looking he waved her phone in the air.

When he climbed in next to her, she reached for the phone and charger and said, "Thank you. I don't know why I forgot it. I'm not normally a forgetful person."

"You've had a lot on your mind."

"I suppose that's true. I'm just so glad it was still there."

As they got closer to home Andrew asked, "Would you like to come with me when I go to collect Cora?"

Bree didn't have to think too hard. If it was between staying home with Mr. and Mrs. Stauffer and going somewhere with her new best friend, the logical choice would be to go with him. "Yes, I'd like that, thank you."

"You'd probably like the singings. They're a lot livelier than the Sunday morning songs and there are so many young people there."

"Sounds good I suppose."

He laughed.

"What's funny?"

"You don't sound enthusiastic."

"It's hard to be excited about anything right now. There are so many things I'm uncertain about, like whether your parents will adopt my baby."

"You're convinced that's the only option?"

"More than anything. I think that's why I met Simon – so I could give my baby a good life."

"The Lord works in strange ways. My parents prayed for another child many times, I'm certain of that. They wanted many more than three children."

"Simon told me that."

"If you believe what you said about God bringing Simon to you, then relax. Everything will work out."

"I didn't say it was God."

He glanced over at her with a frown. "Isn't that what you meant?"

"I don't know if I believe in God; I think there might be some kind of destiny worked out for everyone, or some universal power of some kind, but I'm not convinced about the whole God thing. Simon and I used to talk about it a lot."

He looked at the road ahead. "I didn't know – sorry I just assumed you meant God brought Simon into your life."

"God, the universe, or destiny, it could all be the same thing."

"No! God is God."

Bree kept silent. She didn't want to argue about religious beliefs, nor was she there to convince anyone of anything, particularly when she had no clear idea of what she believed regarding God or spirituality.

When they got home, Andrew stopped the buggy near the front door. "You can get out here, I'll unhitch the buggy up near the barn. We've got about three hours before we need to leave for Cora."

"Thank you, Andrew. And thanks for agreeing to help me."

He smiled and nodded.

When she stepped down from the buggy she

turned around to face him. "Would your parents be home?"

"They usually stay out visiting until late and have dinner at their friends' place."

"Okay." Bree headed to the house, glad that she could relax and be herself. She closed the front door behind her and went into her room. After switching her cell phone on briefly, she checked to see if she had any messages. There were none. She turned it off, and tossed it and the charger into her suitcase and then lay down on the bed. How she wished she could fast-forward a whole year – these next few months were months she wished she could avoid.

She closed her eyes and pretended she was not pregnant, she didn't have to live a lie, and that she was someone else who had a better life.

Chapter 12

Know therefore that the Lord thy God, he is God, the faithful God, which keepeth covenant and mercy with them that love him and keep his commandments to a thousand generations;

Deuteronomy 7:9

B ree woke to loud knocking on her door.

"Bree, do you still want to come with me to collect Cora?"

"Yes. I'm coming." Bree sat up and looked around. She grabbed her pullover from the end of her bed and slung it over her shoulders before she headed to the door. Andrew was already halfway down the stairs. She followed him out to the buggy.

When they were nearly back at the Millers' house, Bree asked Andrew, "Are you going to stay with me? I'm not good with crowds of people."

"Okay, just stick with me."

A time warp was what Bree felt she was in. The

day had seemed to stretch forever; perhaps it was because there had been such an early start. When Andrew had parked the buggy she climbed down, curious to see what the singings were like. Simon had spoken about them as though he'd enjoyed them.

"So it's nearly over?" Bree asked as they stood a distance away from the crowd.

"Won't be long. It'll stop soon. Then there'll be eating and drinking. We've always got lots of food at everything we attend. Then once the night comes to a close, if a boy likes a girl he'll ask to take her home in his buggy."

"Yes, Simon told me a little about the buggy rides and all that. Does Cora like a boy?"

He smirked. "She wouldn't tell me if she did."

"Do you think she does?"

He eyed Bree carefully. "Why? Has she told you she likes someone?"

Bree laughed and looked over at Cora. "No. I've only just met her. See how she is looking to her left a fair bit? Do you think she's looking at the boy with the thick dark hair?"

"No, that's Billy. I know she doesn't like him."

"Why's that?"

"I can't really say except to tell you that they wouldn't be a good match."

"What if it's the boy next to Billy, the one to the left of him? He looks handsome."

Andrew took a step back. "Do you think so?"

Bree nodded. "I do."

"What makes you think he's handsome?"

"He's got a pleasant face."

Andrew laughed. "That pleasant-faced boy is our cousin. We don't marry our cousins."

"Okay, well it can't be him, then. She might be like you, not interested in anyone."

"I hope not. That would be pretty lonely for her," Andrew said.

"So you're lonely?"

He scratched his forehead. "I can handle it, but I wouldn't want my sister be the kind of woman who never marries."

Bree folded her arms across her chest. "What

kind of woman never marries?"

"The ones who've been passed over."

Bree's face soured. "That sounds terrible."

"Probably is, and I don't want that for my sister. I hope she finds a man soon."

"Why? She's so young."

"The longer she waits, the less men she'll have to choose from."

"I can't see it's a good idea. Surely people change all the time and the man she likes when she's eighteen might not be the man she'd choose at twenty-eight."

"God works things out. We trust in God for everything."

Bree pouted. "I don't see how that's trusting in God, but whatever." Bree shrugged.

"Do you want to sit down?"

"I'm fine. I'll just lean against this tree." Bree walked a few paces and leaned against a tree and Andrew stood next to her. "Everyone looks like they're having fun."

"Yeah, they are, it's okay for the young ones."

"You're too old to enjoy yourself now?"

"At a singing—yes."

"What do you like to do?"

He smiled. "I like to take my horse out to the dirt tracks and give him a good run."

"While you're in the buggy?"

He nodded. "I'd like to race him but I don't think he'd be fast enough."

Bree nearly said he had the same liking of speed that Simon had, but since racing cars had caused Simon's death, she stopped her comment before it slipped out. "You could get a faster horse."

He shook his head. "No."

"What else do you like to do?"

"I like doing what we did today, minus all the tears." He laughed, and explained, "I like going out and being with friends. Just simple things like that."

Bree wondered who his friends were because she really hadn't seen him with anyone at the meeting besides that girl with the sick brother. "Cora said one of your friends is sick?"

He nodded. "That's Phillip. He was working for my father, had a fall and got a broken leg."

"That's awful. Did your father have insurance and that kind of thing?"

"Yes, he has to have all that." He laughed. "You sound like a lawyer."

Bree gasped. "That would be the last thing I'd want to do with my life, but I suppose living with them has influenced my way of thinking."

"I'd imagine being a lawyer would be a good way to help people."

"I guess, but I've seen the bad side of it. My parents were continually stressed about making partners at the law firm where they worked. When they both got to be partners, they had different kinds of stresses. It's such a horrible cycle."

"It wouldn't have to be that way, would it?"

"You trying to talk me into being a lawyer?"

He laughed. "I'm trying to figure you out. Isn't that what friends do?"

"I suppose so in a way."

"Would you like something to eat now?"

Bree looked over to see everyone milling around the two food tables. "I am a little hungry."

"Come on then." Bree walked over with Andrew to look at the food. He took a plate. "I'll fill it up for you."

"That'll be good, thanks." She was pleased because she didn't know what most of the food was and wouldn't have put much on her plate. Bree looked around for Cora and saw her talking to two boys and a girl. "What about those two boys?" Bree whispered to Andrew as he piled food onto her plate.

He looked around. "Either of those two would be a possibility."

"Which one do you prefer?"

He laughed. "It's all the same to me, I'm not the one marrying them."

"But you'll have to see a lot of him at family events and things like that."

"If I'd have to choose, I'd say the taller of the two. He's Verne. His parents joined us when he was a small boy."

"Interesting; and what's the name of the other one?"

"He's Daniel, the youngest of eight boys."

"And you think he's spoiled or something because he's the youngest?"

Andrew handed her the plate of food. "I haven't thought about it for long enough. You asked me to choose, so I chose Verne for no reason in particular."

Bree looked down at the plate. "Thank you."

"Something to drink?"

"Yes please. Anything, I don't care what it is."

"Follow me."

Bree followed close behind hoping no one would talk to her. Things looked fairly safe, as all the young people were huddled together talking in groups. They looked as though they couldn't have been less interested in why she was a visitor to the community. Maybe it was because she was with Andrew that they left her alone.

When Andrew had poured them a drink each, he saw she had both hands holding the full plate. "I'll hold your drink. Let's sit over here."

Andrew was striding towards a bench seat under a tree and Bree hurried to catch up with him.

"I can take the drink now," she said as she was seated. After she placed the plate of food onto her lap she reached her hand out for the drink.

He smiled at her when he handed the cup to her.

"And how old are you when you stop coming to the singings?"

"Around twenty-five. I'd say twenty-five was getting too old. Were you in love with the father of your baby?"

Bree nearly choked. She hadn't expected him to ask such a thing. "I thought I was, but I wasn't. That's what scares me. How do I know my own mind?"

"If you don't know your mind then there might be a chance that you would decide to keep your baby, and if that's the case then maybe you should tell my parents the truth now."

Bree swallowed hard. "I couldn't. It was such a wicked thing I did to have them think it was Simon's child. To turn around and tell them it wasn't, would be too hurtful for them. I thought you said to leave things as they were for now."

"It would cause them some pain, I'll agree with you there. It might be a case of better some pain now than a lot more later on."

"That's not why I came here, Andrew. I only want to do good. I want the best for my baby and it would be good for your parents too."

"I know. I'm just thinking through all the things that might go wrong."

"Why don't you pray to your God that nothing will go wrong and everything will turn out well?" She smirked at him, which caused him to smile widely.

"I'll do that. Thank you for that reminder."

Bree laughed, and then she placed a morsel of food into her mouth. Cora caught sight of them and waved and Andrew gave a wave back.

"She looks happy. I never remember being happy like that," Bree said when she swallowed her mouthful.

"Never? You've never been happy even once in your life?"

She looked into the night sky. "I was happy around Simon. We used to play video games together and watch movies. And when I was very young my parents used to spend Christmases on Ryan's family estate. It was on a lake and we did a lot of swimming and playing. Ryan's got two older sisters and it was good to hang out with them." Bree stared at Andrew.

"See? You have had happiness."

"I guess I have had some."

"Someone once told me happiness is a decision."

"I've heard that too. The old saying about the glass can be half empty or half full and it depends on whether you look at something as being good or bad."

"That's a good comparison. I think it's true. Nothing's all good or all bad. Maybe things are just the way we look at them. You could be upset about your situation or pleased that you're having a baby, and the decision whether you keep the baby or adopt the baby out is all yours. Nobody is forcing you to do anything. Your parents aren't saying you must keep the baby or you must do this or that. Surely that's a good thing."

Bree nodded. "I do have my own choice about things. That's true; I feel better. Keep going. Tell me some more things to feel good about."

Andrew raised his eyebrows and laughed. "Okay. Let's see. You have a new friend – me. You're staying at a house where you have been welcomed, and you have options regarding your future."

Bree opened her mouth to speak, but hadn't noticed Cora had walked over to them. "I'm ready to go now."

"Gut," Andrew said. "We'll just wait for Bree to finish."

Bree drank the last mouthful of drink and then looked at the food on her plate. "I'll be quick. You shouldn't have given me so much, Andrew."

"I'll help out." He proceeded to help her eat the finger food on her plate. When all was gone, he took the glass and her empty plate from her. "I'll just take these back and then we can go."

When he left, Cora said, "How long have you two been here?"

"We came at the end of the singing. It looked like fun." Bree lied, it didn't look like fun at all. It looked quite boring. Her idea of fun was eating pizza and watching movies, not sitting around with a group of people singing.

"It is fun. You should come next time."

"Maybe," Bree said. "If I'm not too tired."

Cora sat next to her and looked over at her brother. "He's talking now. He'll most likely be a while. He does like to talk." Cora sat where Andrew had been sitting. "What did you do today?"

"Your brother was nice enough to take me somewhere so I could charge my cell phone."

"You've got a cell phone?"

"Yes. Everyone's got one. Everyone I know has got one."

"I was going to go on *rumspringa* and the first thing I would've done was get my own phone, but now I'm too scared to leave home after what happened to Simon."

"I imagine that would've turned you off."

"Tell me what it's like away from the community."

Bree smiled. "There's electricity for one thing, and all the women wear makeup and lots of women wear jeans, but you'd know all that."

"What's it like to have electricity?"

"Flick a switch and it's there – light, cold or heat, television, radio, and pay TV. It's not that easy without it. It's like going back to the way my great grandparents used to live."

Andrew waved a hand in the air.

Cora said, "Looks like he's ready to go."

Chapter 13

Knowing that a man is not justified by the
works of the law,
but by the faith of Jesus Christ, even we have believed
in Jesus Christ,
that we might be justified by the faith of Christ, and
not by the works of the law: for by the works of the
law shall no flesh be justified.
Galatians 2:16

When they got home, Mr. and Mrs. Stauffer were still not home; the house was in darkness. Cora struck a match and lit a kerosene lamp that was by the door, and then proceeded to turn on the main overhead gaslight in the living room.

"Is it unusual for them to be so late?"

"They've been this late before."

"I might go to bed now," Bree said.

"Take this with you." Cora picked up the kerosene lamp and handed it to her.

"Thank you. I guess I'll need this."

"Good night, Bree."

"Night, Cora." Bree trudged up the stairs, suddenly feeling very tired. She pushed open her bedroom door and placed the light on the nightstand. When she heard noises outside, she hurried to look out the window. It was Andrew doing something with his horse. She stared down at him and by the light of the moon she saw a handsome well-muscled man. Growing fond of Simon's brother was definitely not in her scheme and she wasn't about to ruin her plan. If Simon's parents adopted her baby, she'd be able to walk away knowing everything would be all right.

Bree recalled the only advice her mother had given about men: there were nice rich men and nice poor men so why settle for a nice poor man?

That had been her mother's sales pitch for Ryan. The only thing was that Ryan was not a nice man, but at least Bree had found that out sooner rather than later. Bree hoped that her parents would not tell Ryan about the child she was carrying. Ryan just might put two and two together and realize the baby had to be his.

* * *

Bree was pleased when she woke early the next morning, without anyone else having to wake her. The sun was only just peeping over the horizon.

She turned on her phone to check for messages, but still, there were none. As she switched her cell phone off, she felt guilty for turning it on in the house after Andrew had asked her not to. Sick and tired of feeling either guilty or mad with herself, she changed into a dress, brushed her hair and headed downstairs. At the bottom of the stairs she was faced with Andrew, who looked as white as a snowstorm.

"Bree! I was just on my way up to let Cora know that I'm heading out to look for *Mamm* and *Dat.*"

"They didn't come home?"

He shook his head.

"I'll tell her."

"Denke. I'm going now." Andrew turned and headed out the front door, then seconds later, Bree heard the sound of rapid hoofbeats.

Bree walked into the living room and collapsed onto the couch wondering where they could be and what might have happened to them. She was nibbling on her fingernails when Cora ran down the stairs.

"Where's Andrew going so fast?"

"He said to tell you your parents didn't come home last night and he's going to look for them."

Cora's mouth fell open. "Did he call anyone?"

Bree shrugged her shoulders. "I don't know. That's all he said, he was in a hurry."

"I think they were probably too tired to travel home and stayed at someone's house."

"Has that happened before?"

Cora shook her head.

"I'm sure they're all right."

Cora nodded. "I'll fix you some breakfast."

"I'll help," Bree said as she pushed herself up

from the couch.

Bree tried her best to keep Cora's mind off what might have happened to Mr. and Mrs. Stauffer.

It was an hour later when Andrew came home followed closely by his parents' buggy. Cora ran out to meet them.

Mrs. Stauffer stepped down from the buggy looking ghostly pale, like she hadn't slept a wink.

Bree stood at a distance, staying near the front door, and heard Mrs. Stauffer say, "We were at Henry and Ruth's house when Henry had a heart attack right in front of us. They didn't have a phone to call out so your *vadder* had to run to the Millers' *haus* next door. Then Henry was gone before any help could reach him. He died right in front of us. We stayed the night with Ruth."

Cora put her arm around her mother. "Come inside."

Bree didn't know what to do or say. She felt like an intruder at that moment. She hurried back to the kitchen and sat down. When Cora guided Mrs. Stauffer into the kitchen, Bree said that she was sorry about her friend and Mrs. Stauffer nodded politely.

"Can I do something, Cora?" Bree asked.

"Nee, you just finish your breakfast."

When Mr. Stauffer and Andrew came into the kitchen, Bree felt she should make herself scarce. She was at a loss to know what the appropriate thing would be to say to everyone.

* * *

A week later, Simon's family was attending another funeral and this time they were joined by Bree. They entered the Fullers' house, where the body had been laid for people to pay their last respects. Bree hung back and stood just inside the front door. She'd never seen a dead body before and she didn't feel the need to see one now.

"You okay?" Bree looked up to see Andrew.

"Yes. I just don't like funerals." Bree knew that the whole thing had been hard on Andrew's mother, seeing Mr. Fuller drop dead just weeks after her son had died tragically. She'd been in bed with a headache two days straight when she'd come home from Ruth Fuller's house on that Monday morning.

"Not many people do. We'll be heading to the graveyard soon."

"That'll be good. I need some fresh air."

He took hold of her arm. "Come outside now. You don't have to stay inside if you don't feel well."

Once the sunlight reached her face she felt better. "I didn't want to appear rude. I'm not sure how all the rules go."

"We don't have rigid rules about things."

Bree nodded, while thinking that Andrew was so entrenched into the Amish way of life he didn't realize just how many rules he was following.

When more people followed them outside, Andrew said, "Come over to the side. They'll be bringing the coffin out soon."

"Is that the buggy it's going in?" She pointed to a large buggy that looked like it'd been made for carrying coffins.

"*Jah.* Then we'll all follow it to the graveyard."

There was such a sense of formality and tradition associated with the Amish that Bree knew the members would have a sense of belonging to something larger than themselves. That was something she'd missed out on in life – belonging to something or someone. She looked down at the bump under her dress and hoped her baby would be happy with the decision she'd made. Her baby would belong to a loving group of people and never know loneliness like she'd known. One thing she knew for certain was that her baby would never be called a mistake.

Bree stood still next to Andrew as four men carried the coffin out of the house on their shoulders. They lowered the shiny wooden coffin into the buggy.

More people came out of the house, and then Andrew said, "Okay, let's go."

She walked with him to his father's buggy and she traveled with Andrew's family as they fell in line with the funeral procession. The buggy with the coffin led the way followed by a long trail of buggies.

It brought back memories of Simon's funeral, but then she'd been an outsider, and now she felt like she was somehow a part of Simon's family. They didn't have far to go before they were getting out of the buggy once more.

The crowd gathered around the open grave while Bree stood back. The bishop spoke words about life and death. When he ended his words by saying that now Henry Fuller was safe in God's house, chills ran up and down Bree's spine. How good it would be if what the bishop had said was all true. What if there really was a loving creator who cared for everyone individually? Whether it was true or not, it did seem to give all the Amish people some hope.

Bree looked on as the men lowered the coffin into the grave. Out of the corner of her eye she saw someone lift his head. It was Andrew; he was now walking over to her.

"You okay?"

Bree knew he was concerned. "Yeah. It's just a bit sad. Someone's alive one minute and the next they're gone."

He nodded. "I know. It's hard not to be a little fearful of the unknown."

Bree was certain he was going to give her a spiel about how believers were better off with God, but how would it be better to be dead? "How's your mother handling it?" Bree asked. "Everyone was so quiet in the buggy I was too afraid to say anything."

"I'm sure Simon's death has all come back to her since we're all at another funeral so soon. As the bishop said, death is a part of life and it's something we accept as being a cycle. We're born and then we die."

Glancing up at the sky, Bree said, "That's something no one can escape. No matter how rich they are."

"You thinking about your parents?"

Bree gave a small laugh. "I try my best not to

think about them, but I still find it hard to believe they sent me away."

"Maybe they've had time to cool down and think things through. Perhaps they see things differently now."

She shrugged her shoulders. "Who knows?" One thing was for certain, Bree didn't want to find out. She was not going to risk hearing one more time what a disappointment she'd been to them since she'd been born.

"I'll go with you back to your place if you still want to go. You mentioned collecting some things from your parents' house."

"Would you?"

He nodded.

"I should do that soon. Thank you. Maybe some time next week?"

"You let me know."

"What happens now? Is it over?" Bree asked.

"We go to Mrs. Lapp's house to eat. There's always food after a funeral. Mrs. Lapp is a good friend of Mrs. Fuller."

She stared into Andrew's eyes.

He laughed. "What is it that you're thinking?"

"You've been such a good friend to me since I've been here. Thank you. I haven't had many great friends."

"I told you I'd be your new best friend."

Bree knew their friendship had developed into something genuine and Andrew was not being kind to her out of a sense of duty alone.

* * *

They arrived home late in the evening on the day of Mr. Fuller's funeral. Mr. and Mrs. Stauffer went straight to bed while Andrew tended to the horse and buggy.

"Has your mother got another headache?" Bree asked Cora when they sat together in the kitchen.

"It seems like it. She's not been herself ever since Mr. Fuller died. I was going to spend a couple of days with Susan, a friend of mine, but I thought

Mamm might feel a bit off for a few days."

"I can understand that. It must have been an awful shock to have the poor man die right in front of her."

Cora stood up and headed to the stove. "I'll make us some hot chocolate."

"Thank you. That sounds good."

Just as Cora had placed the third cup of hot chocolate on the table, Andrew came through the back door that led into the kitchen. "Ah, hot chocolate. Do we have marshmallows?"

"Jah, we do." Cora reached onto a top shelf and pulled down a jar of pink and white marshmallows. When she sat down, she pushed the jar over to Andrew.

When Bree saw Andrew's face light up, she smiled. "You have a sweet tooth?"

"I guess I do." He shook four marshmallows into his hot drink and stirred them. "Would you like some?" he asked, looking across at Bree.

"I'll try some."

He pushed the jar over toward her. "You've

never had marshmallows in hot chocolate?"

"Never."

"You don't know what you're missing. Put at least two in and let them melt."

When Bree took two out, she offered the jar to Cora who shook her head. "They're too sweet for me."

Bree picked up her spoon, stirred the marshmallows, and then watched them melt.

"Now take a sip." Andrew brought the hot chocolate to his lips.

After Bree watched him she took a sip herself. "Mmm. It is delicious."

"I know. I can't believe you've never tried it."

"I don't normally have hot chocolate at all. I used to be a coffee drinker before … well, before it made me sick to drink coffee."

"I think it's horrible to have the marshmallows," Cora said. "It's much better plain."

When Cora finished her drink she went to bed leaving Andrew and Bree sitting at the table. Bree was glad to be left alone with Andrew. If things in her life had been different, she would've liked a man such as he. She wondered how she looked to him by the soft glow of the overhead gaslight.

"Are you okay?"

She nodded. "Yes. I am. You're teaching me some important things in life. Like how to drink hot chocolate. Although, it looks like you're eating yours you've got so many marshmallows in there."

He looked into his drink. "Only four. I would've had more, but I knew Cora would've turned up her nose at me."

Bree laughed at him. They talked for at least another hour before Bree thought she should call it a night and go to bed.

Chapter 14

As the cold of snow in the time of harvest,
so is a faithful messenger to them that send him:
for he refresheth the soul of his masters.
Proverbs 25:13

A ndrew waited in the taxi while Bree walked up to the tall fence that surrounded her parents' house. She walked through the front gate, glad that they'd left it unlocked as they normally did. Once she was around the back of the house, she reached up into the side of one of the hanging planters and retrieved the back door key. Staring at the key, she couldn't believe that they'd kept it in the same place. Had they hoped she'd return? They didn't seem too keen to keep her out. She hurried to the door, put the key in the lock, and heard a click as it unlocked.

Bree pressed the alarm code in. It was two - zero – one - one. It was twenty for her mother's birthday and eleven for her father's. Once she had punched the numbers into the keypad, she hurried along the hallway to her parents' bedroom.

She rifled through drawers hoping to find some money, well aware that the meter of the taxi was ticking over. Hopefully she'd at least find enough money so Andrew wouldn't have to pay for the taxi fare. Then at the back of her father's sock drawer she found a roll of notes. She sat on the bed and quickly counted them out. It was five thousand dollars. *That should be enough to pay my doctor, and everything – I hope.*

After she stuffed the roll of notes into a Chanel bag she'd grabbed from her mother's collection, she headed to the door. Before she got there, she smelled a faint waft of perfume and remembered her mother's collection of expensive perfumes she kept on display in her dressing room.

Now standing in front of the perfumes, she grabbed a bottle of something that looked good, pulled the cap off, and sprayed it in the air a couple of times and then walked through it. Her mother had often applied perfume that way, but had never allowed Bree to go near her collection. Just as she was putting the perfume back she saw a letter. She picked it up, turned it over and saw that it was from Ryan. *Why's he writing to my parents? I need to find that out.* She stuffed the letter into the Chanel purse with the cash. Whatever he had to say to her parents had to be something to do with her.

Pleased with her newfound freedom, armed with a bundle of cash in a designer purse, she hurried down the hall, and then flicked the alarm back on. She was careful to replace the key exactly where she'd found it and then she hurried back to Andrew who was waiting in the taxi.

"Did you get what you were after?" Andrew asked when she got back into the taxi.

"Yes. Everything was right where I left it."

"Good." Andrew had the taxi driver take them back home.

When they got back to the house, and the taxi was heading down the drive, Andrew said, "Before we go inside. I want to ask you to come somewhere with me."

Barely able to keep a smile from her face, she asked, "Where?"

"To a horse auction."

"I'd love to. When is it?" Truth was, she would've gone anywhere with him.

"It's next week."

"Okay. Are you going to buy a horse?"

"*Dat's* horse is getting a bit old and we'll need to retire him soon."

"How do you retire him?"

"Don't look so worried. We don't have him killed or anything."

"I've heard a lot of bad things about what happens to horses when people retire them. Glue factory, dog meat, that kind of thing."

"No." He shook his head. "My family would never allow that to happen. Our horses are like our dogs, they're pets."

"That's good to hear."

"He'll graze in our paddock for the rest of his days. Anyway, we don't need to replace him just yet, but it doesn't hurt to look. If I see a good horse going cheap I'll buy him." He smiled at her. "I'm glad you're so kind to animals. That shows you're a good person."

"Was there any doubt?"

He laughed. "No. There was never any doubt. You were a good friend of Simon's so that tells me enough right there."

* * *

The next day Marie had another of her headaches, and Cora had stayed overnight at a friend's house.

Joel asked Bree, "Are you able to look after Marie today? She won't cause you concern, you'll just need to rewet her washcloth when it's dry and take fresh drinking water up to her. I don't think she'll want any food."

"Of course I can. I'll be happy to."

"I would stay home myself, but we've got a deadline for this job. We need to get it to lock-up stage before rain sets in. Rain's forecast for Friday."

"Yes, go. We'll be fine." Bree wondered whether Marie would be able to cope with a baby if she got a headache every time she was under strain or pressure. But if she'd had three children before now, surely she had a way of coping. Maybe Joel had stepped in to help in the times when she was ill.

Bree went to the kitchen and looked out the window at Mr. Stauffer and Andrew loading things in their wagon. Then her eyes lowered to all the washing up in front of her and she decided to get started with the work; then she'd poke her head through Marie's bedroom door to see if she wanted anything.

An hour later, she pushed Marie's bedroom door open just a little, and whispered, "Marie."

Marie opened her eyes and managed a smile.

"Would you like anything?"

She took the wet washcloth off her head. "Can you make this cold?"

Bree stepped forward and took it from her. "Okay. Would you like any food or something to

160

drink?"

"No." Marie closed her eyes.

Bree wet the washcloth in the water from the outside tap, which seemed colder than the water that came to the house. Then she raced back to Marie's room. "There you go. I hope it's cold enough."

"Denke," Marie said in a quiet voice.

Bree glanced at the glass of water beside the bed. "Can you drink a little water?"

"I'll try." Marie pushed herself up and handed Bree back the cloth and Bree handed her the glass. She took several small sips, waited a minute and took a few more.

"I'll fill it up and bring it back." When Marie put her head back on the pillow, Bree spread the washcloth onto her forehead.

After she'd taken the glass of water up to Marie, she had the rest of the day stretched out before her and she wondered what to do. Cora and Marie would never have had a break; they would've found something to do. Bree slumped into the couch and

161

picked up The Bulletin, which she soon found out was an Amish newspaper. Since she had nothing else to do, she read it from cover to cover. It told of births, deaths, and who had visited whom, and general information about the Amish people from different regions.

Since Joel and Andrew had a couple of big days of work ahead of them getting the house to lock-up stage, they weren't coming home for the midday meal as they most often did.

Maybe she could cook something nice for dinner. It was the least she could do. Bree headed to the kitchen and pulled out the recipe cards from the bottom drawer. She'd seen Cora read these cards and follow the instructions.

When she had a chicken and several kinds of vegetables roasting in the oven, she remembered the letter from Ryan she had found at her parents' home. Knowing that she'd be able to leave the cooking for a while, she hurried upstairs.

Before she walked into her room, she stuck her head into Marie's room and saw her sound asleep.

After she grabbed the letter from under her mattress where she'd placed it the day before, she slumped onto the bed and ripped the envelope open. It was no letter. It was a wedding invitation. Then she saw Ryan's name and the name of Prue Westfield. He was getting married to Prue Westfield? She'd never even heard of a Prue Westfield. The wedding was a whole three months away.

"Well, I hope you know what he's like, Prue Westfield, whoever you are." She ripped the invitation into tiny pieces and stuffed the pieces into one of the zip sections of her suitcase.

* * *

Marie was learning what a good kind girl Bree was. It was no wonder Simon had fallen in love with her. Bree kept checking on her to see that she was okay, and Marie knew her concern was genuine.

Surely there'd be a way for Bree to keep her baby.

Even though Marie would've loved to have another child to raise, she wanted Bree to experience the joys of motherhood and not be sad every time she thought of the child she had no choice but to give to another.

Bree says she has no choice but to give her baby up, but perhaps Gott will work on her heart and she might be able to live with us. We'll support her and Simon's baby. Together we can be her family.

She knew her husband and her children were fond of the young woman who was carrying Simon's baby. Bree had fit so well into their family in such a short space of time, and she wasn't even Amish.

More than anything, Marie hoped and prayed that she'd listen to God's call and open her heart to Him. Then all would turn out well for Bree.

It hadn't escaped Marie's notice that there was an attraction between Bree and her eldest son. But that wasn't surprising since Bree had fallen in love with Andrew's brother. Perhaps in time Bree might even open her heart to love again, and Andrew and

Bree might marry. Things between them certainly seemed to be heading in that direction even if only in a small way.

Marie had kept quiet about her observations. Her husband would never have noticed anything between Bree and Andrew, and it wasn't right to discuss anything like that with Cora. Marie was happy to quietly keep an eye on the two of them and watch what developed. Perhaps God had a grand plan in bringing Simon's baby to them beyond them knowing their grandchild.

"Are you certain you don't want anything else?" Marie turned over in her bed to look at Bree. "You can come sit by me and talk if you want to."

Bree smiled, and sat on the side of her bed. "I have the dinner cooking, but I've got a few minutes before I have to check on it again."

"You don't have to be nervous around me."

"I always feel nervous around adults. I suppose I'm one myself, so I shouldn't be."

"You're having a baby, so you are an adult," Marie said.

"I suppose you're right."

"I'm truly glad you've come to stay with us, Bree. I was just thinking how well you fit in with our family."

Bree's face lit up. "Really?"

"Yes, we're all glad you've come and we're happy about Simon's baby."

"I'm so happy to hear it."

"I wish there was some way for you to keep the baby, but you've still got time to think things through." Marie took a deep breath. Too much talking was making her a little tired. "Don't feel you have to leave the child with us just because you said that's what you wanted weeks ago. Keep your mind and your heart open."

"Thank you. I will do that. I just want to do what's best."

"But, you also have to do what's best for you as well as your baby. You're a person too you know."

Bree rubbed the back of her neck, and then stood up. "I know. I better go back to the kitchen. I don't want anything to boil over on the stove."

Marie watched Bree rush out of the room. She hoped she'd given Bree something to think on. There were so many things Marie wanted to ask about Simon, but she didn't want to upset Bree by doing so. In time, she hoped Bree might be able to answer all the questions she had.

* * *

Cora had arrived home in time to help with serving the evening meal that night. It pleased Bree that everyone had complemented her cooking. Perhaps she could cook again, since it tasted okay and no one had suffered from food poisoning.

Marie had managed to eat a little food, but still hadn't come out of her room.

When Bree went to bed, she thought long and hard about what Marie had said to her. It had never occurred to her to take into consideration any feelings of her own. Marie was right; she was a person too. But if she had to choose between her wellbeing and her baby's, she had to choose her baby's.

Simon's parents had made an impression on her and she was glad she hadn't reacted to how standoffish they'd appeared at first. Now she knew that Simon was right about how wonderful they were. The only thing was, it made the selfish lie that she was telling them all the more dreadful. Andrew knowing her lie was most likely the only thing that kept her continuing with her horrid deception. If he saw that her lie was worth it, he would most likely be right. After all, Simon's parents would have a baby to raise. Was it that important that the baby wasn't really Simon's?

Chapter 15

For unto you it is given in the behalf of Christ,
not only to believe on him,
but also to suffer for his sake.
Philippians 1:29

Andrew parked the buggy along with all the other buggies at the back of the auction grounds.

"Come on; we've got to find a good one before the auction starts."

"Okay you lead the way. Where do we go?" Bree was growing fonder of Andrew every day. She was certain he felt the same. He sought out her company whenever he could.

"All the horses are in the white building, and then they're paraded down there and through to the auction ring when they're coming up for sale."

Bree nodded. "So we're allowed to go in and see them?"

He gave a laugh. "Yes. We need to have a look

at them up close."

She hurried to keep up with him as he went on to explain, "They have all their details written next to their stall, their age and whether they're broken to harness or not, things like that. And we can look at their teeth and look at their legs up close."

"Do you get a chance to try them out?"

"You mean like a trial period? Take them for a couple of weeks?"

Bree nodded.

"No, but that sounds like a good idea."

"I don't see why you can't do that. How do you know if the one you choose is not lame or something?"

"You can tell that, if you're experienced, by the way they walk and carry themselves."

"I didn't know there would be so much to it."

"It's not that hard. It's fairly straight forward," he said as they stepped into the building where all the horses were.

The smell of musty hay and horse manure wafted under Bree's nose. "Oh, it doesn't smell good in here."

"I'd have to disagree. I think it smells good. I love the smell of fresh sweet hay, and the horses smell good too. They do to me, anyway." After he glanced at Bree's face, he said, "Do you want to wait outside, or will you be okay?"

"I'm okay." Bree liked how attentive Andrew was toward her. He was always asking how she was and making sure she was all right. "Are you looking for a particular color?"

"No. I don't care what color."

"I'm just asking because all the horses you've got are bay, aren't they?"

"That's right, but it wasn't planned that way. I guess that seems to be the most popular color for Standardbreds, which is what the buggy horses mostly are."

They wandered down the rows of horses and every now and again Andrew stopped to read the description when a horse caught his eye.

"Have you got a favorite yet?" Bree asked.

"Not yet. What about you?"

"I'm sorry to say I'm no judge of horses."

"It takes time, the same as anything. Once you've been around them for a while you'll know what to look for in a horse."

After they wandered around looking at all the horses, they took a seat and watched the auction take place. Andrew hadn't picked a horse that he liked at all, which made Bree wonder if he'd only asked her there as an excuse to spend time with her.

They made a game of guessing how much each horse was going to sell for and Bree surprised herself by being more accurate than Andrew.

"I just let you win," he said when the auction was over.

"No you didn't. I won fair and square. And that means you have to be my servant for a week."

He laughed. "We made no arrangement like that beforehand."

"The winner chooses what they want."

"Ah, you're making up the rules as you go along."

Bree laughed. "I would like you to do something for me."

"Seems I'm always doing things for you. Covering up your secrets, and taking you places. What would you have me do now?"

"Would you take me to see my doctor next week? We'd have to go by taxi. I'm just too nervous to go on my own." Bree cringed hoping he'd say he'd go with her.

"Of course, I'll go with you. Not into the room with the doctor, though."

Bree laughed. "No. You can wait in the waiting room."

"Sounds easy to me."

"Then, you'll do it?"

"I will. Let's go." He took her hand and pulled her to her feet.

Bree knew she was falling for Andrew, but if her feelings got stronger how would she be able to walk away? It was hard enough to walk away from her baby, but at least she'd know her baby would have a good life. Maybe Marie was right;

she shouldn't make up her mind so rigidly about things. Even after weeks with a Godly family she still didn't know if their beliefs were founded in fact or fiction. If only it were true that there was a God who cared. It certainly sounded too good to be true.

* * *

Weeks had passed and Bree's baby was only two weeks from being born. She was certain that she'd fallen in love with Andrew, but she was still confused about many things. Andrew had taken her to the doctor twice, and even though they'd been to many social events with Cora tagging along, she'd still found quiet moments when she was alone with Andrew.

Bree was beginning to think that she had been drawn to the Stauffer family for a different reason other than having Simon's parents adopt her baby. Maybe God had brought her there to marry Andrew so they could start a family together; it seemed too good a thing to hope for. Nothing good had ever happened to her and it was silly for her to think things would suddenly start working out well for her.

"I'll get it." Bree rose from the table and walked to the door when she heard someone knock.

Mr. and Mrs. Stauffer letting her answer the door was just a simple thing which made her feel a part of the family. She expected to see one of the Amish people she knew standing there, but she opened the door and came face-to-face with Ryan. As she covered her mouth and gasped, she took a step back.

After her initial reaction, she stepped forward hoping the family wouldn't learn who Ryan was. "What are you doing here?" she hissed. After a quick glance over her shoulder, she stepped onto the porch and closed the door behind her.

He folded his arms over his chest and looked down at her large stomach that she couldn't cover up. When he looked back up at her face, he said,

"Your mother told me about the baby."

"What do you care? I heard you're going to be married soon anyway."

"I'm going to get custody of the baby. That's what I'm doing here. You can't possibly raise it; you don't even have a job."

"Firstly my baby's not an 'it,' and it's not even yours," she lied.

"I know the baby's mine and I'll order a paternity test to prove it, if I have to."

Bree knew that he'd go to any lengths to get what he wanted.

Mr. Stauffer flung the door opened and stood there while he looked at Ryan, obviously wondering who he was and why he was there. His eyebrows pinched together as he looked at Bree. "Do you know this man?"

Bree put the palm of her hand on her forehead. She was about to be found out to be a big liar. Ryan had ruined her hopes and dreams and now Mr. and Mrs. Stauffer would lose their chance to be parents, or at least grandparents.

Before Bree could think of something to say, Ryan stared back at Mr. Stauffer. "I'm the father of the child she's carrying."

Chapter 16

I will go in the strength of the Lord God:
I will make mention of thy righteousness,
even of thine only.
Psalm 71:16

Mr. Stauffer's eyes opened wide. He looked from Ryan to Bree. "Is this true, Bree?"

Bree couldn't speak and neither could she look at Mr. Stauffer. Before Ryan had come, her life was working perfectly. She was certain that Andrew was falling in love with her just as she was falling in love with him. Now Andrew's parents would never trust her again. The wickedness of her lie was so great she knew the only thing left for her to do was leave the Stauffer house. She had to get out of their house quickly.

If only Andrew had been home, he would've known what to do and he could've calmed his parents.

"Bree, is this true?" Mr. Stauffer asked again.

All she could do was nod as tears flowed down her cheeks.

Ryan chimed in, "Get your stuff, Bree. You're coming with me."

Staring at him open-mouthed, all she could do was hurry past him and head up the stairs. What other choice did she have? She couldn't stay there now that they knew the truth of her lies.

When she was halfway up the stairs, she noticed that Mrs. Stauffer and Cora were walking out of the kitchen so she climbed the stairs faster. She got into her room and threw all her belongings into her suitcase and closed it. *Where are you, Andrew? You'd know what to do.*

The last thing she wanted to do was face all three of them downstairs. Mr. and Mrs. Stauffer and Cora all would know by now that Simon was not the father of her baby. Her lie had been well intended, but now that it was known it seemed an horrendous lie.

Bree picked up her suitcase and headed down the stairs hoping to avoid awkward questions and seeing their hurt faces.

At the bottom of the stairs Mrs. Stauffer looked at her with tears in her eyes. "Is what this man is saying true, Bree?"

All Bree wanted to do was sit down with her and explain what she'd done, and why, but guilt prevented her from doing so. "It is. I'm sorry for the pain I've caused everyone. I wish I could explain." She walked out the door, avoiding meeting the gaze of Cora or her father.

By this time, Ryan was at the bottom of the porch stairs. "Let's go," he said, as he grabbed her suitcase out of her hands.

Bree saw his red sports car and hurried over to it. She slumped down in the seat and then, when they drove away, Bree turned back to look at the house. The three of them were staring after her, Mr. and Mrs. Stauffer and Cora. When Dusty sat down next to the three of them and watched her leave, Bree covered her face with both hands and cried; she'd betrayed the trust of the only people who had ever really cared about her.

After five minutes of solid crying, she calmed down enough to speak. "How did you find me?"

"It wasn't easy; your parents had no idea where you went. I had to have a private investigator track you down."

"How did he find me?"

"Through your phone. Apparently you were turning your phone on and off, and when you turned it on he was able to pinpoint your location. I didn't think he was right, but here you are." He gave her a sideways glance. "What were you doing with Amish people?"

Now she was angry with herself for turning her cell phone on to check her messages. Andrew had asked her not to turn it on in the house. If she'd been respectful enough to listen to him, she wouldn't be in Ryan's car right now.

"Well? What were you doing there anyway? Why were you staying with those people?"

She pressed her lips firmly together and remained silent. She was angry with Ryan, but more than anything she was mad at herself.

"Answer me. I'll find out anyway even if I have to get the investigator on to it."

"It's really none of your business and I'm not going to talk to you. Anyway where are you taking me?"

"Back to your parents' house."

"That'll be a waste of time because they've kicked me out."

"They've changed their minds now that they know the baby is mine. They are adamant that I shouldn't go through with my wedding now with you having my baby."

"My baby shouldn't make any difference to you."

"Legally, you're wrong. I have just as much say about the baby as you do, and probably more so since I have more money to raise a child than you. Your parents think strongly that I should marry you."

She shook her head. "That'll never happen. Go and marry Prudence or Prunella or whatever her name is."

"It's just Prue."

"Well go and marry Just Prue and leave me be."

He scratched his chin. "Prue and I have talked about it and there's every possibility she might be open to adopting the child."

"Never in a million years would I allow that to happen."

"My child is heir to a fortune. I'm not taking this lightly. I need a child to make my parents happy. They won't care about the circumstances of the birth like your parents seem to."

Her baby was just a tool for her parents and even for Ryan, but to the Stauffers her baby was someone to love and to care for, a gift from God, they said. That was something that Ryan and his family, and also her parents, knew nothing about.

As she was figuring out how to get away from her parents, she remembered that she'd left all the cash she'd stolen from them at the Stauffers' house.

"Are you going to tell me how you knew those people? You seemed pretty friendly with them, answering their door as though you belonged there."

She looked out the car window. His words were true; she did feel she belonged there more than any other place she'd lived.

"I have other means of finding out."

Turning back to face him, she said, "They're just friends of mine."

"I don't believe that and you know I'll find out sooner or later so you might as well tell me."

"They let me stay there. I had a good friend called Simon who died and they are his family. They were letting me stay until the baby was born."

"Simon? I think I remember you mentioning a Simon."

She was surprised that he knew who Simon was. "And why are you suddenly getting married to someone I've never even heard of? Is she one of the women you were cheating on me with?"

"I told you. We never had an exclusive relationship."

"You could have fooled me. Well, you obviously did fool me. I just assumed we did."

"We never talked about it. You never asked me if we were exclusive."

Bree put her hand up to put a stop to that topic. "Just don't say any more about that. I suppose Prunella's parents are rich? Richer than mine?"

"I told you it's not Prunella and yes her parents are comfortable. Yes, far more comfortable than yours."

"Ha! I knew it! You wouldn't marry for something like love."

"Don't be so old-school, Bree. Love is a transitory thing; any intelligent person knows that. People fall in and out of love all the time. It's not something that's supposed to last, otherwise it would be a boring world."

When he smiled at her she wished he wasn't so handsome. Someone so horrible as he was didn't deserve to look so good.

"I knew you'd have a grand scheme. I knew it as soon as I read the invitation. The worst thing is that I had anything to do with you in the first place."

He laughed in a low mocking tone.

Bree closed her eyes and prayed to God to get her out of the mess she was in and to find wonderful parents for her baby. While she was at it, she prayed that Simon's family would be comforted and wouldn't be too upset by the way she'd deceived them.

Ryan made her jump when he said, "Here we are."

The second she opened her eyes she saw her parents' house.

Chapter 17

Let no man despise thy youth;
but be thou an example of the believers,
in word, in conversation, in charity,
in spirit, in faith, in purity.
1 Timothy 4:12

Her mother came running out to meet them. "Bree, we were so worried about you."

Bree stepped onto the pavement. "Mom, you and Dad kicked me out."

"We were shocked, that's all. Now we've had time to calm down and think things through we're happy to be grandparents even though I'm far too young." She giggled loudly, and then looked across at Ryan. "Bring her things in, will you, Ryan?"

"Yes, Judith."

"Is Dad home?"

"No. He had an important meeting. I had to postpone some appointments to be here with you when you got here. Come into the house."

They walked in the front door and Ryan followed.

"You knew I was coming? Are you in this with Ryan?"

"Ryan wants to marry you," her mother whispered. "This will work out well if you just do what I tell you to do."

Defeated, Bree slumped onto the leather couch in the living room and waited to see what Ryan and her mother would say to her. Her mother sat opposite her, and when Ryan sat beside her mother, they both stared at her.

"What?" Bree asked.

Her mother turned to Ryan. "Do you want to tell her?"

Bree sat forward. "Tell me what?"

"You and I are getting married, Bree."

"What?" If Bree could've stood up quickly she would've. Her extra weight kept her rooted to the couch. "That's not what you said in the car. What about Prudence?"

"I wasn't serious about what I said in the car. I was just seeing how you'd react. The truth of everything is that Prue refused to marry me when she found out you were having my baby."

"You're not marrying her now?"

He shook his head.

"See, Bree? Everything is going to be perfect."

"Isn't that going to embarrass you, Mother? Everyone will know that Ryan was going to marry someone else, and he only wants to marry me now because of the baby."

"That'll be old news next week. People have short memories for that kind of thing. Anyway, you'll marry Ryan as soon as you can."

Bree pulled a face. Was this what God wanted for her and her baby? It was definitely not what she wanted.

"What do you say, Bree?" Ryan asked.

"I say no. That's what I say." Bree stood up and as soon as she did, her mother stood too.

"You'll do what you're told, young lady."

"You can't make me marry him. I'm going to my room." As Bree hurried off to her room she wondered what they'd do now. Could they force her to marry him? She opened her bedroom door, stepped through and then locked it behind her. Adoption was her best choice, but that was awkward now that Ryan knew he was the father. Realistically she'd never be free of Ryan now that he knew about the baby.

And now that Ryan knew the whereabouts of the Stauffers' house, the baby wouldn't be safe there. She wanted to scream with frustration, but that would only bring her mother and Ryan running to her room. After she sat on her bed she thought of Andrew. He knew where she lived, so perhaps he would come and find her. That was what she wanted.

A loud knock sounded on her door. "Ryan's gone. Let me in so we can talk."

Bree opened the door.

"You should be nice to him. He's the key to your future, and that kid of yours."

"Your grandchild? Is that who you're talking about?"

Her mother sat down on the bed and Bree sat

down cross-legged.

"I know you're upset with Ryan, but he's your best chance out of this mess you've gotten yourself into."

"I got *myself* into? I didn't get pregnant alone."

"All the same, he's agreed to marry you. You loved him once; you told me that."

"That was before I wised up to what he was like."

"You don't have a choice. You can't expect your father and me to put up with a screaming baby in the house. Once you marry Ryan, you'll have all the money in the world and you'll be set for life." Her mother's face beamed with delight.

"And if I don't?"

Her mother's face darkened into a scowl. "If you don't, then I don't know what will become of you. You can't stay here. Where did Ryan find you?"

"I was staying with some friends."

She stood up. "I don't see that you've got any other choice but to marry Ryan. He's been good enough to offer to marry you and cancel his wedding to that other girl."

"I'm not in love with him, Mom."

"In your situation, love is the last thing you should be worried about. Your father will be home soon and he'll tell you the same as I'm telling you."

"It's not what I want. Can't you see that?"

"Do you even know what you want?"

Bree nodded. She wanted her baby to be raised by Simon's parents, but she couldn't tell her mother that. Her mother wouldn't understand anything about Simon's parents or about the Amish community. "What if I wanted to put the baby up for adoption?"

Horrified, her mother said, "There's no way that Ryan would allow that to happen. You'd need his approval and he'd never give it."

Bree knew her mother's words were true, but they could never make her marry Ryan. She simply wouldn't do it.

"He even talked about trying to get custody of the baby so he and Prue could raise it together."

"He would've been joking about that. She called

off the wedding when she learned of the baby. Do you know that he could file a suit against you as an unfit mother and gain custody? If he found you living in less than a perfect situation just now that could strengthen his case. Who were you staying with?"

"Just my friend's family. They're good people, and they live on a farm."

"You can't trust people like Ryan and his family and that's why you have to be on their side. Marrying him is the only thing you can do if you ever want to have any say in your kid's life."

She stared into her mother's eyes for a moment wondering if marrying Ryan was truly her only option.

"Now you stay in your room and think about it while I go down and order food so it's here when your father gets home."

"I'll think about it."

Her mother looked her up and down. "And when was your last doctor's appointment?"

"I'm due for another visit."

"I'll phone and make an appointment for tomorrow."

"I won't get in at that short notice. I've got an appointment arranged for this Friday coming."

"You won't get in at short notice, but I will. I don't want to wait for Friday. Bill's a good friend don't forget. Unless you changed doctors?"

Bree shook her head. "I haven't."

"Good. We agree on something at least." Bree's mother left her alone in the room.

Hoping that Andrew would come to save her, she walked to her bedroom window and looked out at the road. What would Andrew have thought when he arrived home to see his family so upset? No doubt Mrs. Stauffer would have a migraine over the stress and be bedridden for days. She hoped Andrew was able to help them get over their sadness.

A tiny part of Bree felt better to be home and glad that her mother was finally paying attention to her. But that wouldn't have been the case if it hadn't been Ryan's baby.

What a mess she'd made of her life. Would she have to marry Ryan while forever thinking about Andrew? She tried to imagine a future where she could marry Andrew while giving Ryan limited access to the baby – maybe fortnightly visits, but in reality, it would never work.

She couldn't get her mind off the Stauffer family. Perhaps she should write them a letter to apologize and explain her actions. That would be better than talking to them in person. She'd have trouble looking them in the eyes after she'd deceived them so cruelly.

Knowing her father was due home soon she went down to the living room to hear what he had to say about the whole thing.

She settled herself down with a cup of hot chocolate and had found some marshmallows to add to it. Thinking about Andrew, she sat herself on the couch waiting for her father and trying her best to ignore her mother who was sitting opposite flipping through a fashion magazine.

When her father eventually walked into the

living room, he looked at Bree and a smile broke out onto his face. "Bree! Where have you been?"

It was such a fake response, as though he was genuinely pleased she was there.

"Well, you did tell me to leave, Father."

He scoffed. "We were angry and surprised, that's all. We didn't really mean for you to leave."

Bree knew that was not the case. They'd wanted her to go and the only reason they wanted her back home was so she could marry Ryan. Ryan must've convinced them that the baby was his. "Let's cut through the nonsense, Dad. I'm only here because you and Mom are trying to make me marry Ryan. And it's not going to happen."

He fell into the couch next to Bree and stared at his wife. "You told me you had this all arranged."

"It is. She doesn't know what she wants. It's her pregnancy hormones talking. She'll come around and see this is the best thing for her and the only way out of the mess she's gotten herself into." Her mother stood up and looked at her watch. "Let's go into the dining room; the dinner will be here soon."

They all sat down at the dining table just as the doorbell rang.

"Right on time." Mrs. Fortsworth headed to the door and minutes later came back with three large Styrofoam containers. "Help me put these onto plates, Bree."

Even though the dinners looked like takeout in those containers, once they were placed onto fine china dinner plates they tasted like a meal from a fine restaurant, which was where the food had come from.

As Bree took the steak and vegetables and placed them on plates, her mother whispered, "Don't say anything to aggravate your father. I've got him on board with you marrying Ryan, but he's still angry that you've done this whole thing the wrong way around. You should've got married first."

"Ah, a nice home cooked meal," Bree said sarcastically when they were back at the dining room table about to eat.

"And that's another thing. You should be grateful that you have food on the table. If it weren't for your father and me working so hard you'd have nothing. You haven't worked a day in your life ..."

"I think she gets the idea," her father said to silence his wife.

"I am grateful," Bree said before she closed her eyes and said a silent prayer of thanks for her food.

"Are you feeling ill?" her mother asked.

Bree opened her eyes. "No! I was just taking a moment to appreciate the food."

Her mother shook her head. Bree hadn't been brave enough to tell her that she was thanking God for the food just as she was used to doing before every meal at the Stauffers' house. She already missed the calm and serenity of the Stauffer household.

"We're going to the doctor tomorrow. I'm taking the day off so I can drive you there myself. I want to hear what he has to say. This baby is your ticket for your future with Ryan."

"And what if I don't want to have a future with him?"

Her father snarled. "You got yourself into this

mess, young lady. This is the only answer. You liked him enough to get yourself pregnant, marrying him is the only option you've got."

"You're acting like it's a bad thing, Bree. You probably couldn't have worked this out better if you'd planned it. You'd nearly lost him to Prue."

"She can have him." Bree cut another piece of steak and chewed on it. Why was she getting all the blame, as if she got into this situation by herself? Granted, she was silly enough to think she was in love with Ryan, and to be silly enough to think that he loved her, but it took two to make her baby.

Her mother went on, "You'll be set for life. He's worth millions. You'd be able to have anything you want. A home here, a chateau in France, a vineyard in Italy, an apartment in London, and all the handbags you like, and as many designer clothes as you want. The only thing is you must keep Ryan happy."

"It's his father's money not his," Bree corrected her mother.

"He's the only heir and only son."

Immediately, Bree was turned off her food. "That might be the kind of life that would suit you, Mother, but I'm different from you."

"Stop talking to her, Judith. She'll come around in time," her father said.

Sighing loudly, Bree looked down into her plate. Why wasn't the food horrible? She wanted it to be, but the steak was flavorsome and so tender. There was no use talking to her parents and telling them how she felt. She'd have to go with plan B. Only thing was she didn't know what it was yet; she'd only had a plan A. Tonight she'd have to come up with plan B before she was forced into marrying Ryan. With no money behind her and nowhere to go, things were harder for her than they would've been for most people.

Chapter 18

My tongue also shall talk of thy righteousness
all the day long: for they are confounded,
for they are brought unto shame, that seek my hurt.
Psalm 71:24

The next day in the doctor's waiting room, Bree sat in the chair twiddling her fingers, unable to sit still. She'd been awake nearly all night trying to figure out another plan but she'd come up empty.

"Don't be nervous. Is that why you're fidgeting like that?" her mother asked.

"I guess I am a little nervous this time." The last few times she'd been to the doctor, Andrew had taken her and she hadn't felt nervous at all.

"Don't worry. I'll make sure to tell him that you want a caesarean birth. That's the most painless way and they'll give you lots of meds for the pain."

"I'm not sure that's the way I want to go."

"So, you want horrendous pain, do you?" Her mother was being smart-mouthed as usual.

"Of course, I don't want pain. I'm just wondering about different options; not everyone wants the same kind of birth. Maybe I'd be interested in a homebirth."

"Not in my home you won't." Mrs. Fortsworth laughed and then looked at Bree. "You're serious?"

"It wouldn't hurt to find out about it." She'd learned from Mrs. Stauffer that most of the Amish had been having their babies at home for hundreds of years.

"It's not going to happen. It's not safe. This baby is your ticket to financial freedom and you won't do anything to ruin that." Then her voice got softer and she said, "Oh, Bree, don't you understand that your father and I only want what's best for you?"

Bree nodded not certain of that at all. In fact, she was more certain they wanted what was best for them.

"Marrying Ryan is what's best for you. I must say that you having his baby turned out to be a good thing, otherwise he would have married Prue. He had his wedding planned and he had to break things off with her."

"Wasn't it she who cancelled their wedding?"

"Well, it doesn't matter now. All that matters is that Ryan does love you and wants you and him and the baby to be a family."

"Ryan is a cheater, Mom."

Her mother scowled. "Then I advise you to look the other way."

Bree's jaw dropped open. "You think that's okay?"

"What does it matter? Everything in this world is a negotiation. I've told you that so many times. You have what you want, and in exchange, he gets what he wants. He's the one with the money after all."

"What I want is a husband who loves me and wouldn't want to cheat on me."

"As long as he's discrete about it …"

"No, Mom. I'm not going to live like that."

"Yes, you will." She reached her hand out and patted Bree's stomach. "You've left yourself with no choice."

"Bree Fortsworth." The doctor had called out her name.

Bree stood up and her mother stood as well. Mrs. Fortsworth had already arranged permission that she go into the consultation room with Bree.

After they were seated, the doctor greeted them both, and then said to Bree, "How have you been feeling today, Bree?" The doctor looked over his gold-rimmed reading glasses to stare at her.

Bree wished she'd said no to her mother coming in with her. "I guess I've been okay."

He looked at his notes, and then back up at her. "Still no nausea or any other signs of discomfort?"

"No physical discomfort," she answered as she glanced over at her mother.

"I just don't want anything to go wrong with the birth, Bill. I want to book her in for a C-section," her mother said.

He frowned at her. "Judith, I don't recommend it unless there's a health risk to mother or baby. It's not what I'd recommend."

"But surely if we request one, you'll do one for

us? You did one for me with Bree's birth."

"Medical opinion is something that changes all the time. I don't book C-sections to fit in with people's social lives. Many people want their baby born on a certain date, and indeed many doctors perform them around their schedules."

"If we're paying you, then surely you should do what we ask. We're your customers after all. Aren't you supposed to please us?"

"If you want to proceed along those lines, Judith, then I'm afraid you'll have to find another doctor." He stared at Bree's mother. When she remained silent, he continued, "Bree's a healthy young woman and there's no reason she can't deliver this baby with minimal intervention. Sometimes it's a case of the more we interfere the more things can go wrong."

Judith scowled. "You've changed what you used to believe, then."

He chuckled. "Experience is often our best teacher."

"I don't want to have a caesarean," Bree said to

the doctor. "My mother wants me to have one."

"Very good. I'm glad we're singing from the same hymn sheet, Bree," he chuckled again quietly.

Bree smiled. She was starting to like this doctor more and more. Anyone who could stand up to her mother was someone she liked. "What do you think of homebirths?" Out of the corner of her eye she could see her mother glaring at her.

The doctor's thin line of a mouth turned down at the corners. "I think all births need to be in a hospital environment for safety's sake."

That wasn't really what she wanted to hear.

"Even when a pregnancy has gone well, things can happen at the last minute. The baby could get into distress and in cases like those we'd need to perform an emergency C-section."

"See? I told you," her mother said. "Where on earth do you get these strange ideas?"

She wanted to tell her mother to keep quiet, but instead Bree shook her head and ignored her.

The doctor stood up. "I'll take your blood pressure and check you over."

When the visit was over they walked out of the office and headed to the car.

"Well, that went well. Except for the fact that he refused you a caesarian, but I'll keep trying to talk him into it," her mother said.

"No you won't. It's not what I want. And if Ryan's so concerned about me and the baby, where is he?"

"He'll be there when the baby is born. That's all you need to concern yourself with. Now, let's get you home."

When they arrived home, Bree closed herself in her room. Her baby was due any time and she had to get out of marrying Ryan.

She heard the doorbell chime, and looked out the window to see a taxi drive away. Hoping it might be Andrew come to save her, she hurried the best she could to the door so she'd reach it before her mother.

She was greeted at the bottom of the stairs by the sight of her mother holding up a Chanel bag. Squinting she saw it was the same bag she'd taken from the house. "Where is he?"

"I'm calling the police," her mother said.

"What?" Bree asked in horror.

"This Chanel was stolen from the house. Do you know the man at the front door?"

Bree walked straight past her mother and when she got to the front door she saw Andrew's smiling face.

Chapter 19

For the which cause I also suffer these things:
nevertheless I am not ashamed:
for I know whom I have believed,
and am persuaded that he is able to keep that which I
have committed unto him against that day.
2 Timothy 1:12

She was so pleased she hurried to him and flung her arms around him. He encircled his arms around her and held her tight. It was then that she knew he felt the same about her.

"I've come to take you home," he whispered in her ear.

"Who is this Bree? You're making a fool of yourself."

Bree let go of Andrew and turned around to her mother.

Andrew stepped forward before Bree could say anything. "I'm sorry. I should have told you my name. I'm Andrew Stauffer." He held out his hand to shake but Mrs. Fortsworth turned up her nose.

"A lady always offers her hand first. If she doesn't offer it, a man shouldn't reach out his hand like that." She looked him up and down. "I can see that you have no idea of etiquette."

"I'm happy to learn of such things. But knowing nothing about etiquette, my instincts would've been that you would've ignored my blunder and shaken my hand."

"Mother, you're being horrible."

She held up her Chanel bag. "This money and this bag were stolen from the house weeks ago. What's he doing with them?"

"Now you have them back and there's no money missing. Well, not much. Anyway, I took them, not Andrew."

"Who is this man, Bree?"

"He's the man I'm leaving with."

"What do you mean? He's Amish or something, isn't he?"

"He's Andrew Stauffer, Mom. And I've been staying with his family and now I'm going back to stay with them." She looked at Andrew and wondered if his parents wanted her to come back.

"Do you need to bring anything with you, Bree?" Andrew asked calmly.

She closed her eyes for a quick moment. Now she knew what a leap of faith was. When she opened her eyes she said, "I'll get some clothes and throw a few things in a bag."

"I'll wait outside."

"Don't leave without me."

He smiled. "I won't."

She hurried upstairs to collect her clothes, with her mother walking behind her trying to talk her out of going. Finally, when she'd stuffed some clothes into a bag, she turned to her mother. "Mother, thank you for everything you've done for me. I'll come back and visit you."

"What are you doing? Your baby is due any day. And what about Ryan?"

"I'm not going to marry Ryan." She walked past her mother and headed downstairs. When she opened the front door her heart leapt when she saw

Andrew's face.

"Let's go home," he said.

Chapter 20

I have not hid thy righteousness within my heart;
I have declared thy faithfulness and thy salvation:
I have not concealed thy lovingkindness
and thy truth from the great congregation.
Psalm 40;10

In the taxi on the way back to the Stauffer house, Bree asked Andrew, "Do your mother and father forgive me?" When Andrew smiled, she knew they had forgiven her.

"I explained the entire situation to them and they understand your reasons for telling them what you told them about Simon."

"I don't know how they could ever forgive me."

"They do forgive you, Bree, they do. We've missed you. I've missed you." He reached for her hand and she placed her hand in his.

"I've missed you too, and Cora, and your parents. I've even missed Dusty. It was a dreadful lie I told them. I don't see how they could ever forgive me."

"If someone forgives you, you just accept it."

Bree nodded. "I'll try to."

He squeezed her hand. "You'll figure it out."

She stared into his eyes pleased he'd come to rescue her just like a hero from a fairy tale. He was her knight in shining armor.

He glanced at her stomach. "The baby's bigger."

She laughed. "I've not been gone that long. Anyway, the doctor says the baby's only an average size. Wouldn't want the baby to be any bigger."

"My mother's missed you."

"She has?"

He nodded. "We all grew used to having you around. Bree, I asked you once before, and this time, I mean it from my heart. Will you marry me?"

Bree giggled. "You really mean it?"

"I do."

"But I'm not in your community."

"You could be."

"I have been thinking more about God, and everything. I even thank God before I eat, so I suppose I must believe in His existence."

"Does that mean yes?"

"Andrew, I just walked out on my old life to come with you. It meant yes when I did that."

He smiled, put his arm around her, and pulled her close to him. She leaned her head against him and closed her eyes. Now she felt as though things would work out for her.

* * *

It was two weeks later that the Stauffer family members were waiting at the hospital for Bree's baby to be born. Marie had been hurt when she'd found out that Bree had been lying about having Simon's baby, but when Andrew had come home, he explained the whole thing. Bree's intentions had been to leave the baby with them, so she'd been intending to do a good thing.

Now Bree was talking to the bishop about joining their community. Andrew and Bree wanted to marry and in Marie's opinion that would make their family complete. They'd lost Simon, but Simon had brought Bree into their lives.

At the last minute, Bree had developed toxemia and the doctor had advised she have a caesarian section. She wasn't happy about it, but they'd all prayed and then she'd felt more confident. Marie glanced over at Andrew who was pacing back and forth. They'd been waiting for two hours before the doctor came out to them.

"It's a girl, and they're both doing fine."

Everyone was relieved.

"When can I see her?" Andrew asked.

"Come with me. She's able to see one or two of you."

"You go by yourself, Andrew. We'll see her tomorrow," his father said.

Andrew hugged Cora and his parents, and went to see his fiancée.

* * *

Bree was relieved that her baby had finally arrived into the world, safe and healthy. It didn't matter that the birth hadn't gone how she'd planned; she was delighted that her life had worked out in such a short space of time. The best thing was now she could keep her baby, and know that this beautiful little girl would be loved and cared for. She and Andrew were going to be married. All she had to do was become a full member of the community and in a few months she and Andrew and the baby would become a proper family.

She'd kept in contact with her mother, and her mother had told her that Ryan was now denying he was the father, which suited Bree just fine. She wondered if it had anything to do with the baby being a girl. With him denying his paternity, he wouldn't want visitation rights. Of course, she would someday tell her baby the truth of who her birth father was. Bree was well and truly through with lies. She hoped to have some kind of relationship with her parents.

She looked down at the precious baby in her arms

and understood the pain Marie felt at losing Simon. The love she had for her baby was overwhelming. She couldn't imagine living through a loss such as Joel and Marie had lived through, and to lose Simon on his *rumspringa* was doubly tragic.

"Are you ready for a visitor?" a nurse asked.

"Yes." Bree looked up to see Andrew walking toward her. "It's a girl," she said. "Andrea Simone. Named for my two best friends."

He leaned down and kissed Bree on her forehead, and then stared at the baby. "She's beautiful, just beautiful."

Tears streamed down Bree's face.

"Are you okay?"

She nodded. "I'm just happy. I didn't know I could be so happy. Before I knocked on the door of your parents' house, I had nothing and no one in my life, and now things in my life are perfect."

He smoothed her hair away from her face. "You never have to worry about anything ever again. I'm here to look after you and our baby. Our house will be finished soon after we're married."

She stared up into his brown eyes. Their house was being built on the Stauffer's property, not far from where they'd first met when he'd saved her from the bull. "I love you, Andrew."

"I love you too, Bree. I look forward to the day we'll be husband and wife."

She closed her eyes as he kissed her on her forehead. Now she knew without a doubt that God was real. How else would her life have turned out so perfectly?

Now faith is the substance of things hoped for,

the evidence of things not seen.

Hebrews 11:1

* * * * * * * * * *

Thank you for your interest in
Their Son's Amish Baby

To join Samantha Price's
email list and be kept up to date with
New Releases and Special Offers:
click here

Other books in *Expectant Amish Widows* series:
Amish Widow's Hope
The Pregnant Amish Widow
Amish Widow's Faith
Amish Widow's Proposal

****

If you are enjoying this series,
you might also enjoy
Samantha Price's *Amish Baby Collection:*

The Gambler's Amish Baby

What would be worse than being a widow, expecting a baby and trying to run her farm alone?

Libby Wagler was soon to find out. Libby wished for nothing more than her brother's return from *rumspringa.*

Brock Harding won half a farm in a poker game. What will he do when he visits the farm to be faced with an angry Amish woman?

Libby wants nothing more than for the man who cheated her brother to get off her farm.

However, with the farm failing, could a bad mannered, rough looking cowboy be Libby's answer to prayer?

The Promise
Abandoned
Amish Baby Surprise
Amish Baby Gift
Amish Christmas Baby Gone

Samantha Price loves to hear from her readers.

Connect with Samantha at:

samanthaprice333@gmail.com

http://www.twitter.com/AmishRomance

http://www.samanthapriceauthor.com

http://www.facebook.com/SamanthaPriceAuthor